STAR WARS®

THE CLONE WARS™

Grievous Attacks!

"Rookies" adapted by Veronica Wasserman
"Downfall of a Droid" adapted by Tracey West
"Lair of Grievous" adapted by Rob Valois

Grosset & Dunlap • LucasBooks

GROSSET & DUNLAP
Published by the Penguin Group
Penguin Group (USA) Inc., 375 Hudson Street, New York, New York 10014, USA
Penguin Group (Canada), 90 Eglinton Avenue East, Suite 700,
Toronto, Ontario M4P 2Y3, Canada
(a division of Pearson Penguin Canada Inc.)
Penguin Books Ltd., 80 Strand, London WC2R 0RL, England
Penguin Group Ireland, 25 St. Stephen's Green, Dublin 2, Ireland
(a division of Penguin Books Ltd.)
Penguin Group (Australia), 250 Camberwell Road, Camberwell, Victoria 3124,
Australia (a division of Pearson Australia Group Pty. Ltd.)
Penguin Books India Pvt. Ltd., 11 Community Centre,
Panchsheel Park, New Delhi—110 017, India
Penguin Group (NZ), 67 Apollo Drive, Rosedale, North Shore 0632, New Zealand
(a division of Pearson New Zealand Ltd.)
Penguin Books (South Africa) (Pty.) Ltd., 24 Sturdee Avenue,
Rosebank, Johannesburg 2196, South Africa

Penguin Books Ltd., Registered Offices:
80 Strand, London WC2R 0RL, England

The publisher does not have any control over and does not assume any responsibility
for author or third-party websites or their content.

This book is published in partnership with LucasBooks, a division of Lucasfilm Ltd.

Library of Congress Control Number: 2008034013

ISBN: 978-0-448-45003-2   10 9 8 7 6 5 4 3 2 1

TABLE OF CONTENTS

Rookies

CHAPTER ONE

The war in the Outer Rim continued to escalate. The Jedi generals and their ever-dwindling clone army were spread out across the galaxy, and new clones, called rookies, were being rushed into service to support them. The Republic was using every resource it had in its fight against the Separatist Alliance. These rookie clones, manning a network of tracking stations, were all that stood between the Republic and imminent invasion.

Aboard the Republic flagship *Resolute*, Jedi generals Anakin Skywalker and Obi-Wan Kenobi patrolled the galaxy in search of the ruthless General Grievous. The Jedi feared that Grievous was planning an attack, but they did not know where, when, or how he would strike. For weeks, the diabolical general had eluded them. Grievous was clever, cunning, and a master of strategy. He could attack from anywhere.

General Grievous, commander of the Separatist droid armies, was as highly skilled as he was merciless. Half alien and half metal, he had the strength and agility of a machine, but within his artificial body beat a remorseless heart that would stop at nothing to see the Jedi destroyed.

Obi-Wan entered the war room of the *Resolute* and found Anakin leaning on the holo-table, brooding over a holographic map. His astromech droid, R2-D2, was beside him as always.

"Still here, Anakin? When was the last time you slept?" asked Obi-Wan.

Anakin had not slept much since they had begun the search for Grievous, and Obi-Wan was concerned for his friend. The two had known each other since Anakin was a child, and Obi-Wan couldn't help but worry about him. Of course, Anakin did make it easy for him to worry. Stubborn and impulsive, Anakin often let his emotions guide him. But there was no doubting his Force abilities. The Force was strong with him and he made an exceptional Jedi Knight— despite his unorthodox ways.

R2 let out a long, worried beep. He was

concerned for Anakin, too. But the young Jedi was determined and would not rest until Grievous was found.

"I'll sleep after we find Grievous. Clone intelligence spotted him in the Balmorra system, but that was weeks ago. Since then, he's vanished," said Anakin, frustrated.

Obi-Wan rubbed his beard thoughtfully. "Well, unlike you, maybe he's getting some much-needed rest."

Admiral Yularen approached the Jedi with news of an incoming transmission from clone Commander Cody. R2 plugged himself into the holo-table and a hologram of Commander Cody appeared before them.

"Cody. How go the inspections?" asked Obi-Wan. Commander Cody and Captain Rex had been tasked with inspecting the Republic tracking stations to ensure that all were operating at peak efficiency. The Republic couldn't afford any weaknesses.

"The tracking station at Pastil is fully operational. Captain Rex and I are proceeding to the outpost in the Rishi system," reported Cody.

"Good," replied Obi-Wan. "Report back once you've arrived."

The mention of the Rishi system only made Anakin want to find Grievous that much quicker. The Rishi outpost was particularly important to the Republic's survival in this war, and with Grievous still on the loose, there was no telling what might happen.

Just south of the Rishi Maze lay the planet Kamino. It was there that the Republic produced the clones for its army. Hatched, grown, and trained at the planet's facilities, it was the closest thing the clones had to a home. If the droids somehow made it past that outpost, they could easily launch a surprise attack on Kamino and destroy the production of clones forever. The Republic Army would be lost.

"Don't worry, Anakin," Obi-Wan said, seeing the Jedi's concern. "If General Grievous comes anywhere near this quadrant, we'll know about it."

CHAPTER TWO

The Rishi moon had a thin atmosphere and a rocky, crater-pocked surface. The Republic outpost, perched on the rim of one of the moon's many deep craters, was the only sign of life on the stark and desolate lunar plain. There was a landing platform, a crew module, and an array of antennae. But all in all, it was a lonely sight.

A single clone trooper stood sentry on the landing platform. With his macrobinoculars, he scanned the distance, but as usual there was nothing out of the ordinary to see.

"This is the deck officer checking in," he said into his comlink. "There's nothing to report."

Inside the outpost, several clone troopers hung around the base's control center. Some just sat staring at the blank security monitors. Others arm wrestled or just talked.

A battle-scarred clone entered the room. He looked around at the others disapprovingly.

"Attention," one of the clones called out. "Sergeant on deck!"

"At ease," Sergeant O'Niner ordered. "Even though you are all new here, I shouldn't have to remind you that this quadrant is the key to the Outer Rim. If the droids get past this station, they can surprise attack the facilities where we were born on our home world of Kamino."

The clone troopers all nodded soberly. They knew what was at stake.

"There are some officers on the way," the sergeant continued. "So I want everything squared away for inspection. Understood?"

"Sir, yes, sir!" all the clones responded in unison.

Just then, something strange appeared on one of the scopes.

"Sir, incoming meteor shower!" the clone monitoring the scope called out.

"Raise the shield," the sergeant ordered as the clone troopers hurried to their stations.

Outside the outpost several small meteorites tore

across the sky and smashed into the outpost's shields, vaporizing instantly. However, a few managed to get past the shields and slam down on the surface of the moon, creating giant craters in the ground.

Inside one of the smoke-filled craters, a small droid landing pod came to a rest.

Back on the landing platform, the clone trooper scanned the horizon with his macrobinoculars. In the distance he could see the droid pod.

"What the . . ." he said as he moved to activate his comlink.

But before he could report back, a droid head rose into view. He dropped the binoculars and saw four frightening commando droids surrounding him. Another droid came up from behind and hit him in the back with a shock-stick. The clone screamed as he fell to the ground.

Six more commando droids climbed out of the pod. They raised their weapons as they charged toward the outpost.

"Get those doors open," the droid captain called out.

"Roger, roger," they all replied in unison.

"CT-three-two-seven, report in," Sergeant O'Niner called into his comlink. "Sentry, do you copy?"

"Interference from the meteors?" a trooper asked as he manned the control console.

From the outpost viewports, the clone troopers looked out at the landing platform for the sentry.

"I don't see him down there, Sarge," a trooper called out.

O'Niner pointed at two of the clones. "You two," he said. "Go find him."

The two clones grabbed their helmets and walked toward the blast door. As the door slid open they saw six commando droids creeping toward them from down the corridor.

"Droids!" they yelled. This was the first time that they'd seen a real droid and they were caught off guard.

They turned to run back into the control center, but before they could make it back, the droid captain opened fire. The two clones dropped to the floor. Dead.

One of the clones hit an alarm button on the console. They needed to alert the fleet to send reinforcements. He waited for a moment, but nothing happened. He hit it again—still nothing.

"They've disabled the beacon," he called out.

"Get a message to the fleet!" O'Niner ordered. "We have to warn . . ." But a laser blast hit him before he could finish.

The rookie clones reacted with horror and surprise as their sergeant collapsed to the floor. On the ground, O'Niner struggled to roll over onto his back. He raised his blaster, but one of the commando droids kicked it from his hand. The droid looked down at O'Niner and fired its blaster straight at him.

The commando droids turned their attention to the remaining rookie clones, who rushed back to the control room. One of the clones hit a panel and the blast doors slammed shut. He popped open the control panel and ripped out a handful of wires.

"That should slow those buckets down," he said as one of the other clones opened a small hatch that led into a maintenance tunnel.

"This way! Hurry!" he said, and a shower of sparks came from the blast doors. The droids were cutting their way through.

By the time the droids had cut their way into the control room, the clones were gone.

"Four clones escaped, Captain," a droid reported.

"They don't matter," the captain replied. "Hard-wire the all-clear signal and contact General Grievous."

CHAPTER THREE

Just outside the Rishi system, a massive Separatist fleet prepared for invasion. There were dozens of well-armed Separatist frigates and giant Trade Federation battleships moving in formation. A swarm of vulture fighters maneuvered in and out of the larger ships.

General Grievous stood at the bridge of his command frigate. A hologram of the commando droid captain flickered on the console in front of him.

"The outpost is secure, General," reported the captain. "We shut down the alarm and turned on the all-clear signal," it continued.

"Excellent," said Grievous. "Keep that signal alive. I don't want the Republic to find out we're coming."

The hologram faded and Grievous paused for a

moment to consider his imminent victory. With the Rishi outpost under control, he knew that it would only be a matter of time until he would finally be able to destroy the clone-making facilities on Kamino. The Republic Army would finally be at his mercy. Not even the mighty Jedi would be able to stop him.

"Our spy on Kamino is making contact, General," called a droid from the communications console on the ship's bridge.

Grievous's eyes narrowed as he looked over his shoulder at a hologram of the dark assassin Asajj Ventress, one of the Separatist Army's most ruthless commanders. The dark side of the Force ran through her and she was feared throughout the galaxy.

"All the preparations for your invasion are in order," reported the assassin. Her snakelike eyes peered out from under the hood of her cloak. The rest of her dark and sinister face was masked in its shadows.

"Good," responded Grievous. "Our fleet is approaching the system. We are almost at the rendezvous point."

"Very good, my Lord," Ventress continued. "I will await your arrival."

"With the destruction of Kamino, I will stop their

production of clones for good," Grievous laughed victoriously.

It seemed that nothing could stop him.

Unbeknownst to Grievous, the Republic attack shuttle *Obex* approached the Rishi moon. Captain Rex sat at the ship's controls, piloting it toward the surface, while Commander Cody attempted to make contact with the outpost's control center.

"Rishi outpost, this is Commander Cody. Do you copy? Rishi outpost, please respond."

There was no answer.

"Rishi outpost, come in! Rishi outpost, come in!" repeated Cody. He shot Rex a concerned look as he waited for a response.

"Sorry, Commander." A voice came from the comlink.

Cody looked over at the console and saw the image of a clone trooper on the display.

"We're, um, experiencing technical difficulties," the trooper continued.

"This is the inspection team," said Cody.

"Inspection? Negative, negative. We, uh, we do not require inspection. Everything is fine here. Thank you," replied the clone trooper.

"We'll be the judge of that. Prepare for our arrival," ordered Cody as he and Rex exchanged suspicious glances.

"Roger, roger," replied the clone.

Something wasn't right. *There is something familiar about that response*, thought Rex. He narrowed his eyes as he thought about where he had heard it before.

CHAPTER FOUR

Outside the attack shuttle, on the landing platform of the outpost, Cody and Rex looked around suspiciously.

"This is not good," said Rex as they approached the outpost's blast doors. "I don't see the deck officer anywhere."

"I have a bad feeling about this," agreed Cody.

Something was definitely wrong. Suddenly, the blast doors opened and out walked a clone trooper.

"Welcome to Rishi, Commander," he said. His voice sounded like a clone, but his movements were oddly mechanical.

"As you can see, the outpost is operating at peak efficiency," he added. "Thank you for visiting and have a safe trip back."

Rex and Cody were not convinced.

"We need to inspect the base just the same," explained Cody.

As the clone officers continued toward the outpost, the clone trooper moved to block their path. Furious at such glaring insubordination, Rex ordered the clone to take them to the sergeant in command.

"Roger, roger," replied the clone. At the same time, a flare went off in the distance.

Rex didn't need to hear that response a third time in order to realize what was going on. He blasted the trooper, knocking it to pieces. He knelt down beside the remains and pulled off the clone helmet to reveal the commando droid's faceplate.

"Droids," grumbled Cody. "If this outpost has been taken over by battle droids, then that flare must have come from the survivors."

All of a sudden, blaster fire came from nowhere, hitting the ground around them. They were being ambushed by droids! Three of them emerged from hiding, guns blazing. Cody and Rex tried to retreat toward the *Obex*, but two more commando droids appeared from near the shuttle, also blasting away. The air was thick with blaster fire from both sides. The clones ducked behind supply crates and continued to fire back.

"We're cut off!" said Rex.

Two more commando droids emerged from the outpost and threw grenades at them.

"Off the platform!" yelled Rex.

"Copy that," responded Cody.

Just before the grenades hit, the clones used their ascension cables to lower themselves from the landing platform to the crater below. The grenade blast obscured their escape and, as far as the droids could tell, the clones didn't make it.

"Well, *that* sure complicates things," remarked Cody when they were safely on the lunar plain.

In unison, Rex and Cody raised their weapons at the sound of approaching footsteps.

"Hands above your heads!" Rex shouted at the three approaching clones. "Take off your helmets!"

The clones stopped short and raised their hands.

"Sir . . . ?" one of them replied, confused and a little frightened.

"Take them off! *Now!*" ordered Rex.

Rex needed to make sure that they weren't more droids in disguise. The three clones removed their helmets to reveal the familiar faces of clone troopers. Cody and Rex lowered their weapons.

Rex removed his helmet as he looked over the

young clones. "The name's Rex," he said. "But you will call me Captain, or sir."

The rookies snapped to attention. "Sir, yes, sir," they all said in unison.

"And I'm your new boss, Commander Cody," the senior clone announced as he removed his helmet.

One of the troopers identified himself. "My designation is trooper two-seven dash five-five-five-five, sir."

"We call him Fives," a second trooper spoke up. "I'm Hevy and this is Echo."

"Where's your sergeant?" asked Cody.

"We're all that's left," replied Echo.

"Looks like we got ourselves a batch of shinies," Rex said, unimpressed, as he looked over at Cody.

"Shinies, sir?" Echo asked.

"That's right," Rex added. "Your armor is shiny and new. Just like you."

The rookies all looked down over their brand-new armor.

Hevy spoke up. "Sir, my batchers and I are trained and ready. We'll take back our post. Shiny or not."

Rex let out a small smile. "There's hope for you yet, rookie."

CHAPTER FIVE

Aboard the *Resolute*, Admiral Yularen stood at a communication station trying, without luck, to make contact with Cody and Rex. Obi-Wan and Anakin stood beside him.

"Commander Cody, do you copy? Captain Rex, please respond," repeated the admiral.

Although the two clones were supposed to check in once they reached the Rishi outpost, no one had heard from them.

"They should have checked in hours ago," said Obi-Wan. "It appears your captain follows orders as well as you do," he continued with a sly look at Anakin.

Rex was Anakin's second-in-command, and like the Jedi general, he was freethinking and aggressive. It was a combination that at times got them both in and out of trouble. They made an excellent team.

"Perhaps Cody is boring Rex with standard protocols and procedures," replied Anakin, picking up on Obi-Wan's comparison and hinting at similarities between his former Master and the clone commander.

"We need to work on our own boring procedures and figure out a strategy to find Grievous," Obi-Wan reminded Anakin. The lesson: Those boring protocols are sometimes necessary. Always the teacher, Obi-Wan knew that Anakin wouldn't disagree. No one wanted to find Grievous more than he did.

Back on the Rishi lunar plain, the clones moved closer to the outpost. They knew they were outnumbered, but none of that mattered. Retaking the base was their only concern. But first, they had to get through the outpost's blast doors.

Taking a page from the droids' book of tricks, Rex approached the blast doors, walking very mechanically. He was pretending to be the disguised commando droid. The commando droids on guard inside examined Rex through the door eye.

"Unit two-six, is that you?" asked one of the commando droids.

"Roger, roger," responded Rex, trying to mimic a droid voice.

"You sound strange. Is there something wrong with your vocabulator?" asked the droid.

"Roger, roger," responded Rex again, in his best droid impersonation.

But the commando droids were still suspicious. They asked Rex to remove his helmet so they could see his faceplate. Rex grabbed his helmet and moved forward and out of the door's eyesight. While he was out of sight, he took a severed droid head and waved it in front of the door eye.

Watching from beside the door, Cody shook his head. *This is never going to work*, he thought.

A moment later, the door slid open.

Rex and the others charged into the corridor and blasted at the commando droids. The group secured the area quickly and cautiously made their way toward the control center.

"Permission to take point, sir?" asked Hevy.

"*I'm* always first, kid," responded Rex.

Rex moved stealthily up the corridor. In the control room, three commando droids were monitoring different stations while a fourth stood in the doorway, his back to the clones. Rex blasted the droid and the rest the group stormed in firing. The droids returned fire as they scrambled to take cover.

The commando droid captain fired at Rex, but Rex dodged the blast and fired back, blasting the droid's weapon out of its hand. The droid tried again, lunging at Rex with a blade. But Rex was too quick; he rolled out of the way, grabbed the droid captain by its head, snapped its neck, and slammed it to the ground.

Just as the rookie clones began to celebrate what seemed like a victory, Cody noticed a tracking screen filled with tiny little blips. Someone was coming. He ordered the group to the window and the clones followed the commander up to the viewport. There, high above the outpost, the Separatist fleet passed overhead.

"*That's* why they commandeered the outpost. They're mounting a full-scale invasion," concluded Cody.

"We have to warn command," added Rex.

CHAPTER SIX

Grievous stood at a command console aboard the bridge of a Separatist frigate that moved through the airspace above the Rishi moon.

"The Republic base is still transmitting the all-clear signal," the battle droid captain reported to Grievous. "But for some reason our commando droids are not responding."

"We can leave nothing to chance," Grievous growled in response. "That base cannot be allowed to alert the Jedi that we're coming," he continued. "Send down reinforcements to investigate!"

"Roger, roger," the droid captain replied, and ordered a landing ship to the outpost.

Back at the control center, the clones tried frantically to work the communications console. It was no use. The droids had sabotaged the transmitter. There was no way to alert the Jedi. It needed to be repaired, but there wasn't time. Grievous's reinforcements had just landed at the outpost. The clones watched in horror as squads of battle droids and super battle droids marched down the ramp of the landing ship.

"We can't protect the outpost from that army of clankers for very long," remarked Cody.

"Then we'll destroy the outpost instead," said Rex.

If they destroyed the outpost, the all-clear signal would stop. They had a new mission: to protect Kamino no matter the cost. Grievous and his army were just moments from invading. If he succeeded, he could put an end to the production of clones for good. They had to stop him, but they couldn't do it alone. Destroying the base was the only way to alert the Jedi.

"We can use the L.T.!" said Echo excitedly.

The others looked at him quizzically.

"This moon is frozen over for half the year. We use liquid Tibanna as fuel to heat the base," he explained.

"Liquid Tibanna. Highly explosive," elaborated Cody.

All they had to do was move the fuel tanks into the control center and set off a few thermal detonators. That and hold off the army of battle droids that were marching toward the outpost.

Once everyone was briefed on the plan, Rex and Echo headed off to collect the tanks while Cody, Hevy, and Fives raided the weapons locker.

"This one here is mine!" said Hevy, eyeing a massive quad cannon—the largest gun in the locker.

Cody looked at Hevy.

"A big gun doesn't make a big man," he said.

Outside, the battle droids had reached the door.

"Reinforcements reporting. Open up," said the battle droid sergeant into its comlink.

The doors hissed open and there stood Hevy, holding the huge quad cannon!

"You didn't say *please*," he said as he opened fire.

The entire droid squad was destroyed. The rest of the droids on the landing platform reacted quickly and advanced toward the blast doors. Between the blaster fire and Hevy's cannon, the air was thick with laser bolts and explosions. Still largely outnumbered, the clones were only able to hold back the droids for a short while before they retreated back inside the outpost and closed the blast doors.

In the war room of the *Resolute*, Admiral Yularen was still trying to reach Cody and Rex. Anakin and Obi-Wan remained beside him, anxious for a word from the clone officers.

"Captain Rex, come in. Commander Cody, are you there?" continued Yularen.

He turned to Obi-Wan. "General, there's still no response."

"What about the all-clear signal? Is the base still transmitting?" Obi-Wan asked.

"Yes, sir," responded Yularen.

"If something were wrong, they would contact us. We need to focus on finding Grievous," Obi-Wan replied.

Grievous paced frantically across the bridge of the frigate. This mission was taking much longer to complete than he had expected.

"What is the status of the base?" he screamed at the droid captain. "Is it secure?"

"Uh . . ." the droid captain hesitated with his reply. He'd seen what Grievous did to droids when he wasn't happy. "We've run into some difficulties . . ." he continued. "There seem to be a few clones left, sir."

"Then wipe them out!" Grievous roared, almost knocking the droid from his chair. "We cannot let a few puny clones stop us."

The clones' success seemed unlikely. The battle droids had blasted their way through the blast doors. The clones continued to fire back at what seemed to be an endless tide of droids. They knew that if they were going to blow up the outpost, they would have to do it soon. Cody ordered Hevy and Fives to fall back to the control center.

"Rex, ready with those fuel tanks?" Cody called over his comlink. "Time's a-wasting."

"Almost ready," Rex answered.

Cody and the rest of his group retreated down the corridor to the turbolift and met up with Rex and Echo, who had just set the last of the thermal detonators around a stack of liquid Tibanna tanks. It was an ominous sight. Once those tanks exploded, the outpost would be completely destroyed. There was one minor problem, however.

"The handset isn't linking up with the detonator," Rex informed them.

"I'll take care of it," said Hevy, taking the handset from Rex. "It'll be fixed in no time. I'll be right behind you."

Reluctantly, Rex left Hevy behind. Rex, Cody, Fives, and Echo ran into the maintenance hatch. After they had gone, Hevy tried everything he could to link up the handset to the detonator, but nothing would work.

This isn't good, thought Hevy. *There has to be another way.*

Hevy could hear the sound of droid footsteps approaching nearby. Quickly, he grabbed the quad cannon and retreated down the corridor.

Out on the crater, the rest of the group had just settled themselves some distance from the outpost, safely away from the impending explosion.

"Hevy, hit the . . ." began Rex. "Where's Hevy?"

"I'm on it, sir," came Hevy's voice over Rex's comlink.

"Hevy, get out of there!" Rex shouted back.

But he couldn't leave just yet. Over his comlink, from his hiding place in the corner of the corridor,

Hevy explained that the remote still wasn't working. He was going to have to detonate it manually.

Distracted by his conversation with Rex and the others, Hevy didn't notice three battle droids enter at the other end of the corridor. But the droids noticed him.

"Hey, hold on there!" said one droid.

"It's a clone. Blast him!" said another.

They fired at Hevy. Rex and the others could hear everything over the comlink.

Hevy needed their help. They would have to go back for him.

"Back to the maintenance pipe. Let's move!" ordered Cody.

"It's no use. I know what I have to do," said Hevy, still firing back at the droids.

"I don't like your tone, rookie," replied Rex, concerned.

Within the outpost corridor, Hevy continued to exchange heavy fire with the battle droids. He managed to dodge most of their fire, but was suddenly hit from behind. It was a jolt; Hevy had never been shot before. The blast whipped him around and he could see another squad of droids firing at him from the other end of the corridor.

He could hear Rex over his comlink: "Soldier, come in. Are you there?" And then a little more frantically, "Soldier, come in! Respond! Talk to us!"

Hevy wasn't responding. He was kind of busy. He lifted his quad cannon and fired at the squad of droids just before darting into the control center.

The control center was overrun by droids. The battle droid commander was seated at the controls. Hevy aimed his quad cannon and fired at the commander, destroying it along with several other droids that were standing nearby. But all of a sudden the cannon stopped firing. He was out of ammo. Lacking any other options, Hevy threw the cannon at the droids, taking out a few of them. The remaining droids continued to advance on Hevy. He was hit several more times before he finally fell to the ground. Still determined, Hevy used his remaining strength to crawl toward the detonator. The droids stood over him, their blasters pointed.

"Do we take prisoners?" one droid asked another.

"I don't," answered Hevy as he pressed the button on his detonator.

Cody, Rex, Echo, and Fives watched as the outpost went up in a tremendous explosion. The blast destroyed everything, including the Separatists' landing ship and all the surrounding droids. There was nothing left except for smoking ruins. There was no way that Hevy could have survived.

None of the clones spoke for a while. Then Echo finally said, "Hevy always said that he hated that place."

On the *Resolute*, Admiral Yularen noticed that the all-clear signal had stopped.

"The Rishi base has stopped transmitting!" the admiral shouted to the Jedi.

"It must be Grievous," grumbled Anakin.

"Sound the invasion alarm," Obi-Wan ordered to the crew. "Let's get this fleet underway."

The bridge crew sprung into action and within moments, the fleet was on its way to the Rishi system.

From the viewing console on the Separatist frigate bridge, General Grievous's eyes squinted as he stared at the burning outpost in disbelief. He bellowed furiously as he smashed his hands against the controls.

"I didn't tell them to blow up the station!" he growled.

"Isn't it good that the base is destroyed?" asked the battle droid captain, stupidly.

Grievous turned and glared at the captain. Why were droids incapable of being anything but incompetent fools?

"Idiot!" he said as calmly as he could. "The explosion will have destroyed the all-clear signal. Now the Republic will know we're here!"

As if on cue, the Republic fleet appeared in front of Grievous's viewport.

"The Republic fleet," he grumbled. "We're outgunned. Get us out of here."

Through their binoculars, Fives and Echo watched as the Separatist fleet retreated. Hevy had saved them all. Rex also noticed something in the sky above. Two Jedi gunships screamed overhead. Anakin and Obi-Wan had come to pick up the clones. Cody raised his blaster rifle in acknowledgement.

In the hangar bay, Echo and Fives received combat citations from the Jedi.

"On behalf of the Republic, we thank you for your valiant service and we honor your comrade's sacrifice," said Obi-Wan.

He and Anakin bowed to the clones and headed

back to the bridge. Rex looked over the clones. They were battered and dirty.

"Congratulations. You're not *shinies* anymore," he said. "You showed me something today. You're exactly the kind of men I need for the 501st."

"Sir, yes, sir!" responded Fives and Echo in unison.

Anakin stood on the bridge, deep in thought. Sure, things had worked out, but would they be so lucky next time? One thing he knew for certain was that neither the Jedi nor the Republic had seen the last of General Grievous.

Downfall of a Droid

CHAPTER ONE

Three Jedi cruisers hovered over the planet Bothawui. The Separatist Alliance and the Republic Armies had been struggling for control of the Outer Rim. The Separatists, led by General Grievous, outnumbered the armies of clone troopers fighting for the Republic. Bothawui was a key planet in the Outer Rim, and the Republic didn't want to give up control without a fight.

Jedi General Anakin Skywalker was assigned to protect the planet. His ship, the *Resolute*, commanded the fleet guarding Bothawui. Admiral Yularen stood on the bridge. Flanking him were a clone officer pilot and Ahsoka, a Togruta girl whose species came from the planet Shili. The young girl was Skywalker's Padawan, and she accompanied him on all of his missions. She had the dark orange skin of her people and white markings on her forehead and cheeks. Three blue-and-white-striped head-tails called *lekku* grew down her back and on either side of her face.

Admiral Yularen wore the simple blue military uniform of the Republic. He gazed out the windows at the dense field of asteroids surrounding Bothawui. The asteroids streaked across the dark sky in glittering shades of red, but they were as dangerous as they were beautiful.

"Don't get too close to those asteroids, Lieutenant," he warned his pilot.

"Yes, sir," the pilot answered. "Do you really think they're going to show up?"

"If Master Skywalker says they are coming, they'll be here," Ahsoka promised. "Be patient."

Down in the hangar bay of the *Resolute*, Anakin Skywalker was making repairs to his Delta-7B starfighter. Anakin sat in the cockpit of the wedge-shaped one-man fighting craft. His astromech droid, R2-D2, was plugged into the wing socket.

"It looks like we now have the fastest ship in the fleet," Anakin said, checking the readouts on the screen in front of him. "Boost the thrust ratio all the way this time."

"*Beep!*" R2 replied.

R2 was about to obey the order as a small wheeled droid passed by. R2 beeped out a greeting.

"*Braaaaap!*" the treadwell droid answered with a rude burp. The simple droid had a pole-shaped body and eyes like binoculars on top of the pole.

"*Beep, beep, beep!*" R2 said, insulted.

"*Pftttth!*" The treadwell let out another rude noise and then rolled behind the starfighter.

"Are we clear to test the engines?" Anakin called to R2. The astromech droid beeped in reply. "All right, Artoo. Stand by."

The ship's thrusters ignited, sending a big plume of flame out of the rear of the ship. A loud beep of alarm sounded.

Anakin turned to see the treadwell droid, covered with black soot from the thrusters. The little droid toppled over onto its side.

Anakin shook his head. "Artoo, he didn't deserve that!"

R2 answered with a mischievous whistle just as Ahsoka ran up.

"Skyguy, there's an urgent transmission coming in," she told Anakin.

"Ahsoka, don't call me that in front of

everybody," Anakin scolded.

"It's urgent, Master, sir," Ahsoka replied.

Anakin and R2 followed her to the *Resolute*'s war room, where Admiral Yularen waited for them. An image of Jedi Master Obi-Wan Kenobi flickered on the holo-table in the room's center.

"The Separatist fleet commanded by General Grievous is headed your way," Obi-Wan warned.

Just hearing the name Grievous could strike fear in the hearts of most of the Republic's supporters. Grievous hunted Jedi for sport and battled with four lightsabers at once. Recently, his forces had seen victory after victory in the Outer Rim.

"Seems like that coward always knows when and where to attack us," Anakin said thoughtfully.

"You're heavily outnumbered, Anakin," Obi-Wan said. "I advise retreat."

"If we run, the Separatists will take control of this sector," Anakin replied. "I can't let them do that."

"And that is your problem," Obi-Wan said sternly, knowing that his former student liked to take foolish risks.

"Master Kenobi is right," Ahsoka chimed in. "We should regroup. We don't stand a chance against—"

Anakin interrupted her. "Ahsoka."

But Ahsoka could be just as stubborn as Anakin. "Suicide is not the Jedi way, Master," she said, glaring at him.

"You should listen to your Padawan," Obi-Wan advised.

Anakin smiled slyly at Obi-Wan. "As you listened to yours, my old Master? No, we are going to stay and fight." He looked down at the holo-table, at the images of all of the ships and weapons at his disposal. "And I think I know how to beat General Grievous at his own game."

Nearby, six ships zoomed out of hyperspace into Bothawui airspace. The bulky frigates were heavily armed warships owned by the InterGalactic Banking Clan. These days, the ships were used by the Separatists in their war against the Republic.

General Grievous stormed onto the bridge of the command frigate. The general looked more droid than alien, with four metal arms, a metal torso, and metal legs. A skull-like mask covered his face and his living brain, revealing only two cold, yellow eyes. His gray cape swirled behind him as he stormed across the floor.

The battle droid captain turned to face his leader. "Our spies were right, General. The Jedi have positioned a fleet beyond the planetary rings."

Grievous gazed at the green glowing screen in front of him. The droid was right. There was a small fleet of Jedi starships between the asteroid belt and Bothawui.

"Move our ships through the asteroid field to engage them," he replied. His damaged lungs wheezed inside their metal cage.

"*Through* the field, sir?" the captain asked.

"If we attack from above, they will have the advantage," Grievous explained. "So we will go through the rocks."

The droid captain nodded in reply. The large ship led the others through the field of jagged asteroids. There was barely room for them to move between the heavy space rocks.

Clunk! An asteroid bounced off of the hull of the bridge.

"That didn't sound good," the droid captain said nervously.

"All power to the forward shields!" Grievous ordered.

The droid captain looked alarmed. "What if they attack us from behind?"

"They can't," Grievous replied. "The asteroids

will protect us."

Anakin's starfighter and a fleet of V-19 fighters launched out of the Jedi cruiser. They moved in fast to engage the enemy ships.

"Gold Squadron, tighten formation," Anakin ordered from the lead fighter. "Slow approach, let's draw them in."

"Yes, sir," a clone pilot replied as he moved his fighter into formation.

"*Beep, beep!*" R2 called out worriedly.

"Don't worry, Artoo," Anakin said. "Grievous is falling right into our trap."

In the *Resolute*'s war room, Ahsoka stood at her radar screen. Multicolored rings moved across the screen as she tracked the frigates as they moved through the asteroid field toward them.

"*Resolute* command to Gold Leader," she said anxiously. "We are standing by."

A clone officer stood over a radar station and called out the position of the frigates. "Enemy closing to zone six . . . zone five."

The frigate fleet slowly eased toward the edge of

the asteroids. On his screen, Grievous saw a fleet of V-19 fighters flying toward them. One of them was different—Anakin Skywalker's delta fighter. They flew out toward the asteroid belt. Behind them, three Jedi cruisers sailed ahead, moving straight for the Separatist fleet.

If Grievous had a mouth, he would have smiled. The small V-19 fighters were merely a nuisance. He had six ships at his command, and the Jedi only had three. He liked those odds. Already three of his ships had passed safely through the asteroid belt.

"General, we have a clear shot at their cruisers," the captain told him.

"Good, good," Grievous said. He eyed the screen one more time. "Concentrate fire on the closest Republic cruiser!"

The sky exploded as the lead three frigates opened fire on the Republic ships.

CHAPTER TWO

Bam! The *Resolute* rocked as the Separatist ships barraged it with fire. In the war room, Ahsoka struggled to keep from falling as the ship shook violently.

I hope Skyguy is right about this, she thought.

Bam! The *Resolute* took another hit. Two of the clone troopers around her went slamming into the wall. Ahsoka looked at the screen to see the six frigates charging toward them.

"We're outgunned!" she cried into her comlink. "We're not gonna last a mynok minute out here!"

Anakin replied from the cockpit of his starfighter. "Hang on, Ahsoka! We've got 'em right where we want 'em!"

He led the V-19 fighters in formation toward the Separatist fleet. Below them, one of the big Jedi cruisers was hit hard. The ship started to sink down to the planet below.

"It's no good, incoming's too heavy!" a clone pilot called over the comlink.

His warning came too late. The dark sky exploded with white light as one of the V-19 fighters was hit. It careened into another fighter, triggering a second explosion.

"Gold Squadron, take evasive action!" Anakin commanded.

The V-19s broke away and turned back toward the planet. Only Anakin moved ahead, charging at the enemy frigates.

"*Beep, beep!*" R2 said nervously.

"No, Artoo, we're not retreating," Anakin said firmly. "Good thing you gave us that extra power."

General Grievous saw the squadron retreat—and saw victory in his grasp. "Let's finish them off!" he cried.

All six of the Separatist frigates had cleared the asteroid belt now.

Anakin was ready to make his move.

"Ahsoka! They're in position! Unveil our little surprise!"

"Right away, Master," Ahsoka replied. "Rex, old

boy, it's time you joined the party!"

"With pleasure, sir!" Captain Rex replied.

Rex climbed into his huge AT-TE walker. Anakin had strategically hidden the land-walking weapons in the craters and hills of the asteroids. Now a huge army of them lumbered out into the open. Their huge laser cannons were pointed at the Separatist fleet.

"General, we've been outflanked!" the droid captain warned Grievous.

But before the enemy could react, Rex set Anakin's plan into motion.

"All units, fire at will!" he ordered.

Boom! Boom! Boom! The asteroid belt exploded in flares of smoke and light as the AT-TE pilots hit the rear of the frigates, targeting their engines. Grievous's strategy had worked against him—the rear of the ships had no shields in place at all.

One of the frigates went down in a ball of orange flames.

"Impossible!" Grievous yelled.

Ahsoka looked at her screen and liked what she saw. Their fleet had the frigates surrounded.

"Forward cannon, let 'em have it!" she commanded.

The two remaining Jedi cruisers opened fire on

the Separatist ships. Grievous fumed as his frigates were pounded from the front and behind with blaster fire.

Anakin skillfully steered his fighter into the cluster of frigates.

"This is too easy!" he said.

He wove between the frigates, avoiding metal flak flying off of the enemy ships. He flew up against the bridge of Grievous's ship, hitting it with a rapid-fire barrage of laser blasts.

"Get us out of here!" Grievous bellowed as his ship rocked from the blows.

"Uh, where are we supposed to go?" the droid captain asked.

Frustrated, Grievous turned and lumbered off of the bridge. He made his way to the landing bay and hopped into his starfighter. The bay rocked as more blasts from the AT-TE walkers ripped through the frigate's hull.

Grievous made his escape just as the frigate exploded. Anakin spotted the general speeding past him.

"Grievous!" He swiftly turned his fighter around and pursued the fleeing ship. He could see Grievous's fighter light up as the general powered into hyper-drive. If Anakin didn't act quickly, he would lose Grievous for good.

"Hang on, Artoo!" Anakin called out.

He swung his fighter in right behind Grievous and . . .

BOOM! A nearby Separatist frigate exploded in a huge blaze of fire.

"More speed, Artoo!" Anakin urged.

The droid obeyed, and Anakin piloted his starfighter right through the fireball. The delta fighter emerged with a shard of metal lodged in the left wing like a knife blade.

"*Beep beep!*" R2 warned. Sparks flew from the wing.

"See what you can do about that, buddy," Anakin said. He focused on Grievous's fighter up ahead. He had one chance to fire . . .

"Uh-oh," Anakin said. Sparks were flying out of his ship now. Then a plume of fire shot out of the hole in the wing.

"I got a bad feeling about this," he said.

BAM! Anakin's ship burst into flames. He lost control, and the ship spiraled off into space.

CHAPTER THREE

Anakin slowly opened his eyes, squinting under the bright white light. Ahsoka and Rex were standing over his bed, and a silver medical droid hovered next to him. Anakin felt the droid pull a plug out of his arm.

"What happened?" he asked groggily.

Ahsoka nodded toward the clone captain.

"You owe Rexster your skin, Skyguy," she told him.

"Just doing my job, sir," Rex said modestly. "It was your plan that won the day."

"Grievous is AWOL, but his fleet of tinnies is nothing but spare parts," Ahsoka reported cheerfully.

Anakin strained to sit up. "Good work, both of you," he said, looking around. "Where's Artoo?"

A troubled look crossed Ahsoka's face. "I'm sorry, Master," she said softly. "He's gone."

Anakin sank back into his pillow. R2, gone? He let out a sad sigh. R2 was much more than a mech droid—he was a friend.

A short while later, Anakin and Ahsoka gathered in the war room for a debriefing with Obi-Wan. The Jedi's image glowed with blue light on the holo-table.

"Congratulations, Anakin," Obi-Wan said. "Your resourcefulness always amazes me."

Anakin couldn't meet Obi-Wan's gaze. "Thank you, Master."

"You look troubled," Obi-Wan remarked.

"I lost Artoo in the field."

"Well, R2 units are a dime a dozen," Obi-Wan pointed out. "I'm sure you'll find a suitable replacement."

But Anakin wasn't giving up. "I could take a squad down there, track him down."

"Anakin, it's only a droid," Obi-Wan said matter-of-factly. "You know attachment is not acceptable for a Jedi."

"It's not just that, Master. Um . . . how do I put this?" Anakin took a deep breath. "I didn't wipe Artoo's memory."

"What?!" Obi-Wan cried in alarm. "He's still programmed with our tactics and base locations? If the Separatists get ahold of him . . . what possessed you not to erase that droid's memory?"

Anakin couldn't answer. Ahsoka tried to help him. "Master Obi-Wan, sometimes Artoo having that information has come in handy."

"Well then, find that droid, Anakin," Obi-Wan said crisply. "Our necks might very well depend on it."

"Right away, Master," Anakin promised.

Anakin felt a little better, knowing he had a chance to track down R2. He decided to use the *Twilight* for the job. He and Ahsoka had commandeered the old freighter on a mission to the planet Teth. The junker had turned out to be a pretty sturdy ship.

Anakin climbed up onto the rear deck. Ahsoka stood there, next to a gold astromech droid.

"Master! They just delivered your replacement droid," she announced. "This is R3-S6!"

R3 swiveled his dome-shaped head and gave a cheerful chirp.

"I've heard that the new R3s are far faster in thinking skills and more powerful than the old R2 units," Ahsoka said, trying to make her Master feel better about losing R2.

"And best of all, Master, he's gold!" Ahsoka

added. She knew she had to sell Anakin on the new droid. He wasn't R2—but their ship needed a mech droid, whether Anakin liked it or not. "A gold droid for a Gold Leader? Of Gold Squadron?"

Anakin eyed the droid suspiciously. "You can't replace Artoo," he said. Then he walked into the ship without another word.

R3 let out a sad beep.

"Don't worry, Goldie," Ahsoka said. "You'll get to know him later. Come on."

Anakin powered up the ship and steered it out of the *Resolute*'s hangar. The space above Bothawui was littered with debris from the enemy freighters. Chunks of metal floated past them, and Anakin tried to ease his way through without hitting anything.

Suddenly, Anakin spotted something. "There's my ship!" he cried. But his happiness quickly deflated. There was no astromech droid in the port. "Artoo's gone!" he cried. "He must have escaped. He's got to be around here somewhere."

"Artoo isn't on the scanners, but there is a ship out there," Ahsoka reported.

A freighter came into view through the window. The hulking metal ship looked like it had been cobbled together from spare parts.

"Looks like a Trandoshan scavenger," Anakin said. "Probably combing the battlefield for salvage."

Ahsoka had heard of the Trandoshans. "The historical texts say—" she began.

"Archive texts can only teach you a part of the picture, my young Padawan," Anakin said, interrupting her. "You'll learn a lot more through some hands-on experience."

As always, Anakin had a plan. The *Twilight* was the perfect cover for them. They could pass for rogue scavengers. Anakin and Ahsoka donned white ponchos over their Jedi uniforms. Then they boarded the scavenger ship, along with R3.

As soon as they left the air lock, a foul smell hit their noses.

"Ugh! What's that smell?" Ahsoka cried.

"Trandoshan," Anakin told her. "That's Huttese for 'snuffin poodoo.'"

Ahsoka grimaced. She had changed the diaper of a baby Hutt once, and she'd thought nothing could be worse than that smell. Until now.

"You'll get used to it," Anakin said.

A probe popped out of the walls and extended toward them. The probe had what looked like a large eyeball at the end—a camera, most likely.

Anakin gave his most charming smile. "Hey, we'd like to buy a droid. You sellin'?"

The probe withdrew into the wall. A door opened in front of them, and a Trandoshan squeezed through the door. The pudgy scavenger was a reptilian humanoid wearing a long robe. His wide face was covered in scales, and his mouth held rows of tiny, sharp teeth.

Anakin made a face. "Uh, maybe we won't get used to the smell. This one's bad."

The Trandoshan nodded at them. "I am Gha Nachkt, purveyor of previously owned collector's items."

Ahsoka couldn't take the smell any longer. She fell to the floor in a faint. The Trandoshan didn't seem to notice.

"You're in the market for a new droid?" he asked, his yellow eyes gleaming with greed.

"We're looking for an R2 unit," Anakin replied. "You happen to pick any up recently?"

"An R series? No, no, not for a long time," Gha Nachkt said. "R2s are rare these days. Everybody wants them for the war."

Ahsoka struggled to get back on her feet. She still felt woozy.

"We've got some fine T7s," Gha Nachkt went on. "Maybe a protocol droid for the little girl to play with?"

"Little girl? I'll show you . . ." she said angrily, reaching for her lightsaber.

Anakin put his arm around her, stopping her.

"Pookums here really has her heart set on another R2," he said, trying to keep up their disguise. "She lost the last one."

"Pookums? Oh, brother," Ahsoka muttered.

Gha Nachkt looked at R3, and the greedy gleam in his eyes grew brighter. "Nice R3 unit. Trade for a C-14?"

"Not on your life, lizardo!" Ahsoka cried.

Anakin quickly took some credits out of his poncho, making sure the Trandoshan could see them. "Now let's see how much I have here . . ."

Gha Nachkt grinned. "Tell you what. I may have an R2 unit buried somewhere in the hold."

The Trandoshan led them to the salvage bay and opened the hatch. Beyond it was a large hold crammed full of robots, spare ship parts, and mechanical junk.

"Help yourself, but be careful," Gha Nachkt warned. "There are many, uh, unique items down here."

Anakin led Ahsoka into the hold. "Don't worry, my pookums will protect me," he called behind him.

"Right behind ya, gramps," Ahsoka teased.

The hatch closed behind them. Ahsoka and R3 followed Anakin deeper into the chamber. The messy piles of junk cast creepy shadows around them in the dim light. Faint beeps and squeaks could be heard within the piles.

Anakin waved his hand, using the Force to move a pile of junk blocking the way. Ahsoka gasped.

Four gunmetal droids with cylindrical heads stared at them with glowing red eyes.

"Assassin droids!" Ahsoka cried.

CHAPTER FOUR

Ahsoka was prepared to defend herself from an attack—until she realized the droids were plugged into a charging station. Luckily, they were deactivated.

"These must be the 'unique items' we were warned about," Anakin guessed. "These assassin droids can be very unpredictable."

"They're switched off. They don't look so tough to me," Ahsoka said boldly.

"Nothing looks tough to you. Take my word for it. They're deadly," Anakin replied.

"*Beep!*" R3 agreed. Anakin turned.

"Arthree, access the computer and find the inventory manifest," he instructed. "Artoo's gotta be around here somewhere."

"*Beep! Beep!*" The gold droid rolled over to a computer port sticking out of the hull and plugged in.

As R3 worked, a high-pitched whistle pierced the air.

"Did you hear that?" Anakin asked. "That sounded like Artoo!"

Ahsoka wasn't so sure. "How can you tell the difference?"

"It came from down here," Anakin said, dashing down a corridor. It led to a closed hatch.

"Arthree, get this open!" Anakin called behind him.

Arthree spun the interface that was plugged into the computer port. The hatch didn't open, but the overhead lights switched on.

"We don't need the lights on!" Anakin said impatiently.

"No, Goldie! The hatch!" Ahsoka urged.

Anakin drew his lightsaber. "Never mind. I'll do it myself!"

He ignited the lightsaber, and the rod of blue light illuminated the hold. Anakin began cutting through the metal door.

Arthree spun his interface once again. This time, he activated the IG assassin droids! One of the charged droids lunged out and grabbed Ahsoka around the waist.

"Master!" Ahsoka cried.

Anakin spun around and chopped off the droid's arm with his lightsaber. Ahsoka fell to the ground. Anakin used the Force to slam the one-armed droid into a stack of boxes.

"Goldie! Shut those droids down!" Ahsoka yelled.

R3 quickly spun his interface, but it was no use. The other three assassin droids pulled away from their recharging cables and moved toward the Jedi. Anakin quickly helped Ahsoka to her feet.

"I'm afraid that Arthree is a little slow on the uptake," he said.

The three IG droids aimed their blasters at the Jedi. Ahsoka activated her lightsaber just in time to deflect a sizzling red laser blast.

The air sparked with light and heat as Anakin charged forward, deflecting bolts back at the droids with his lightsaber. The hum of Anakin's powerful weapon sounded like a swarm of bees. But the assassins were unharmed by the deflected fire. They dodged Anakin, leaping around the room with their metal limbs. They clung to the ceiling and walls and fired at the Jedi from above.

Anakin and Ahsoka expertly blocked the laser fire.

"Back atcha, piston head!" Ahsoka yelled.

One of the IG droids pushed a crate toward Ahsoka. She cried out as the crate trapped her against the hull. The droid turned to Anakin, his blaster ready to fire.

In a flash, Ahsoka freed herself from the crate. She jumped up into the air, slicing the droid in two with her lightsaber as she landed.

"You were right about the hands-on experience, gramps," Ahsoka joked. "Much better than the archives."

"Good job, but you missed one," Anakin pointed out. The last droid rose up behind him. Without skipping a beat, he destroyed the droid's weapon with one blow from his lightsaber. Then he spun around, cleanly slicing off the IG's head.

Anakin turned to R3. "As for you, Stubby, you'd make a poor excuse for a light switch."

R3 gave a sad beep.

"I'm sure he did his best," Ahsoka said.

"His best to get us killed?" Anakin sounded angry. "Artoo would have *never* made that mistake. Arthree can't even get that door open."

Anakin went back to the hatch and ignited his lightsaber, ready to start cutting again. But R3 spun the interface one more time, and this time, the hatch door opened.

Anakin was hoping to find R2 inside. Instead he found himself face-to-face with Gha Nachkt! The Trandoshan looked surprised, and then his look quickly changed to anger.

"If you didn't have a lightsaber, you'd be a dead man!" he growled.

"Where's my droid?" Anakin asked. He pointed his lightsaber right at Gha Nachkt.

Ahsoka grabbed the lightsaber. "Master, what are you doing? Artoo's not here!"

Anakin realized Ahsoka was right. He turned off his lightsaber and marched past the Trandoshan.

"Let's get out of here," he muttered.

Ahsoka and R3 followed as he stormed toward the air lock. Gha Nachkt shouted after him.

"I told you there were no R2 droids back here! Look at this mess you made! You owe me, Jedi!"

Gha Nachkt stormed to the bridge. He watched and waited until the *Twilight* flew off of his ship's dock. Then he turned to his control station and flicked a switch. A hologram of General Grievous appeared.

"What is it?" Grievous snapped.

"I'm en route to the rendezvous point, General,"

Gha Nachkt reported. "I've got the merchandise you were looking for."

A hidden panel in the wall opened behind him. It revealed a holding cell . . . with R2-D2 inside! The droid was held prisoner by a restraining belt, but he didn't look harmed.

Grievous laughed an evil, choking cackle at the sight of the droid.

"It must be valuable," Gha Nachkt went on. "A Jedi came looking for it! Maybe it is worth more than we negotiated."

"Don't push me, slime," Grievous said. "You bring that R2 unit to me as fast as you can get here . . . or else!"

"Ahh, yes, of course, General," Gha Nachkt replied. "Just kidding."

Behind him, R2 let out a frightened beep.

CHAPTER FIVE

Back on the *Resolute*, Anakin and Ahsoka gathered around the hologram of Obi-Wan Kenobi. Anakin told him about what had happened on the scavenger ship.

"We have to assume that Artoo was destroyed in the explosion that claimed your ship," Obi-Wan said.

"Yes, Master," Anakin said sadly. He still didn't want to believe it was true.

Obi-Wan turned to other matters. "Our intelligence has confirmed that Grievous's spies have been intercepting our transmissions."

"He must have some sort of secret listening post out there somewhere," Ahsoka guessed.

Anakin nodded. "That would explain how he's been able to ambush our fleets."

"Split up your squadrons, Anakin," Obi-Wan

ordered. "Find that base and destroy it."

Anakin hated to give up the search for R2. But this was an important mission. "It's as good as done, Master Kenobi."

"May the Force be with you both," Obi-Wan said as the hologram faded from view.

With Rex's help, Anakin got the clones ready for the mission. The pilots climbed into their V-19 fighters. Ahsoka and Rex stood by as Anakin explained his plan. The gold mech droid, R3, stood behind Ahsoka and watched.

"I'll sweep the outer corridor while the rest of your ships focus on the center," Anakin told Rex.

"Are you sure you want to go it alone?" Rex asked.

"I'm sure," Anakin replied. "More than one fighter will just draw too much attention."

"Yes, sir," Rex said crisply. Then he walked off.

"Master, you'll need a droid to help you navigate," Ahsoka reminded Anakin.

Anakin pointed at R3. "I think Stubby is defective."

"*Eeeooohhhhh*," R3 whined.

"Give him another chance, Master," Ahsoka said. "This is the perfect time for you and him to, you know, bond."

Arthree gave a hopeful beep.

Anakin sighed. "All right. Come on, Stubby."

With a cheerful chirp, R3 rolled toward Anakin's starfighter.

Before long, the V-19s were ready to fly. Led by Anakin, the starfighters flew out into Bothawui space. Each ship flew into a hyperspace ring, which would give them the boost they needed to make the jump into hyperspace.

"Good luck, General. We'll see you back here," one of the clone pilots said over the comlink.

"While you're looking for that listening post, keep an eye out for Artoo," Anakin said.

"Will do, sir," the pilot replied.

Anakin pressed a button, and his fighter zipped into hyperspace. He was determined to find the listening post. And, if he was out there somewhere, he'd find R2.

Back on the scavenger ship, Gha Nachkt snored in his pilot chair. The Trandoshan had left the door open to the holding bay.

R2 scanned the ship's bridge. The coast was clear. The droid rolled back, then quickly sped forward, ramming into a metal post. The restraining bolt popped off of its chassis, clattering to the floor.

Free, R2 quietly rolled across the bridge. He had to find a way to send a message to Anakin. He turned into the nearest corridor.

A dark shadow cast a frightening shape on the walls. R2 looked up and into the glowing red eyes of an IG assassin droid.

"Beep!" R2 quickly wheeled around and headed in the opposite direction. The air lock was just ahead. The IG stalked him from behind, getting closer with each step.

Just before he reached the air lock door, R2 hid in a side compartment in the wall. The IG walked past him into the air lock.

R2 popped out of his hiding place and plugged into the air lock's door control. The IG turned and raised its blaster.

Zip! R2 closed the door before the assassin droid could fire. The IG beeped angrily inside. Then R2 opened the outer air lock door underneath the droid's feet.

"Aaieeee!" The IG droid screeched as it fell into the vacuum of space.

R2 whistled good-bye and turned back toward

the bridge. He bumped right into Gha Nachkt!

"Removed your restraining belt, have you? What were you up to?" the Trandoshan asked. He reached toward R2, an evil smile on his face.

The droid slowly rolled backward, frightened.

Gha Nachkt was scary enough. Soon, R2 would be turned over to General Grievous!

CHAPTER SIX

Obi-Wan had given Anakin some clues as to
the possible location of the secret listening post. As
Anakin zoomed through hyperspace, he checked the
instruments on the control panel.

"Arthree, have you verified those coordinates on
the search grid?" he asked.

From his perch in the wing of the starfighter, R3
replied with a positive beep.

Anakin piloted the ship out of hyperspace. "Okay,
let's see what we can find. Activate long-range
scanners."

"*Beep!*" R3 replied.

Suddenly, an alarm began to ring in the cockpit.
The loud, pinging sound echoed out into space.

"No, not the tracking beacon!" Anakin cried in
alarm. "Shut it down, Arthree! Shut it down!"

Back on the *Renegade*, Ahsoka and Rex heard the beacon over their scanner screen. Ahsoka turned to Rex in alarm. Anakin was calling for help!

"Rex, get ahold of as many men as you can!" she yelled.

"Right away, sir!" Rex replied.

In his starfighter, Anakin frantically flipped switches on his control panel.

"Why do I have to do everything?" he complained to R3.

Finally, the tracking beacon stopped ringing.

"Let's hope Grievous didn't hear that," Anakin said under his breath. But as soon as he said the words, two enemy freighters zoomed into view.

"Yeah, he heard it," Anakin said.

"*Beep beep!*" R3 cried in alarm.

One of the ships fired its laser cannon at the starfighter.

"Time to leave," Anakin said. He piloted the ship away from the freighters. "Plot a course out of here and prep the hyperdrive engines!"

R3's dome head spun from side to side. The droid seemed confused. Then the hyperspace ring clamped open and detached from the ship! It floated toward the Separatist freighters.

"What are you doing? I said prep them, not drop them!" Anakin fumed.

He quickly raced to reconnect with the hyperspace ring. Before he could reach it, the ring exploded in a blast of laser fire.

Anakin grunted in frustration. "Where's Artoo when I need him?"

There was no way for Anakin to escape now. General Grievous watched the hyperdrive explode from the bridge of his command ship.

"Launch everything we have!" he commanded.

"Sir, it's only one fighter. He can't escape," the battle droid captain pointed out.

"Everything!" Grievous bellowed.

At his command, a squadron of gray vulture droid fighters swarmed out of the enemy ships. The unmanned fighters boasted an impressive array of weapons. Now they were all aimed at Anakin.

A storm of laser fire hit Anakin's ship. It rocked violently as he tried to maneuver away from the droid fighters. The lead vulture ship launched two more missiles. Then the other droid fighters did the same. R3 beeped a warning.

"I know, I know! Missiles!" Anakin yelled. He lowered his voice. "I hate missiles."

He quickly sized up the situation. The missiles were closing in fast. The ship wasn't fast enough to outrun them. There had to be some other way . . .

"We're going on the offensive, Arthree. Get ready to cut the engines," he told the droid.

R3 beeped, puzzled.

"Will you just do what I tell you?" Anakin asked impatiently.

The mech droid beeped again, and the engines cut out. Anakin yanked on his controls and the fighter rotated around so that the back was now facing the enemy ships.

"Hit the stabilizers, Arthree," Anakin ordered.

The fighter spun around to face the approaching missiles. Anakin took careful aim at the missile in the lead. He waited for just the right moment, and then . . .

ZAP! A single laser blast shot out from Anakin's ship, striking the lead missile. It exploded in a blast of light, starting a chain reaction that destroyed all the missiles behind it.

"All right, Arthree. Let's get turned around before those fighters catch up to us," Anakin said.

R3 made a beep that clearly meant "Not gonna work." Frustrated, Anakin opened fire on the droid fighters as they closed in. Three of them exploded in flames, spiraling off into space. But there were more than he could handle.

"You know, if this ship blows up, you go with it!" Anakin reminded R3.

"*Beep, beep, beep!*" the droid replied.

"What do you mean the laser guns won't fire?" Anakin asked angrily.

The droid fighters swarmed Anakin now. There was nothing he could do . . . he couldn't even fight back.

"Poodoo," Anakin sighed.

Suddenly, the droid fighters exploded, filling the darkness of space with blinding light. The *Twilight* burst out of hyperspace and hovered in front of Anakin's ship.

"Did somebody call for help? Again?" Ahsoka asked over the comlink.

"Only by accident," Anakin replied.

The *Twilight* opened fire on the remaining droid fighters. From her post in the cockpit, Ahsoka opened the doors to *Twilight*'s cargo bay.

"Cargo bay doors open. You better get inside," she told Anakin.

"I'd love to, but Arthree's having a problem

with the engines," he replied.

"*Beep!*" R3 was insulted.

"Arthree, is everything okay?" Ahsoka asked sweetly.

"*Beep, beep*," R3 replied. He sounded happy to hear Ahsoka's voice.

The engines on the delta fighter roared to life.

"See, you just gotta learn how to talk to him," Ahsoka said. "Let's give him some cover, boys!"

"Yes, sir!" Captain Rex replied.

The *Twilight* let loose a barrage of fire on the droid fighters. While they were busy dodging the blasts, Anakin sped his starfighter into the cargo hold. It was a tight fit. The edges of the wings gave off sparks as they scraped against the walls of the hold.

"I'm inside," Anakin reported. "Now let's get out of here, Ahsoka."

Ahsoka pressed some buttons on the control panel. "Power up, Rex," she said. "We're going right between those tin cans."

Ahsoka steered the ship right between the two large freighters! The ships moved closer together, trying to stop her. They couldn't fire weapons from this angle—but they could easily crush the *Twilight*.

Anakin walked into the cockpit.

"Thanks for the ride. I'll take it from . . ." he stopped, shocked, as he saw what was happening on the screen. "What are you doing?"

"No time to talk," Ahsoka replied.

"It's not gonna be easy," Rex added.

The *Twilight* moved ahead with a sudden burst of speed, clearing the two freighters. The large ships slammed together as the *Twilight* sailed ahead, free.

Ahsoka turned to Anakin and grinned.

"Saved you again, Master."

"Yeah, looks like your training's paying off," Anakin said.

Rex looked at both of them. "Can we get out of here, sir?"

"Hit it, Rex!" Ahsoka ordered.

Rex pulled a lever, and the *Twilight* jumped into hyperspace.

General Grievous watched the ship warp out of view. He was too furious to speak.

"Uh, they got away, sir," the battle droid captain said.

Grievous reached out and swatted the droid's head. It clattered to the floor. The general angrily stormed off of the bridge.

GENERAL GRIEVOUS

Commander of the Separatist droid armies, the ruthless cyborg General Grievous is a highly skilled warlord with a personal vendetta against the Jedi Order. Grievous lives as an alien enhanced by a machine's body, his body parts replaced with robotic appendages that give him superhuman strength and agility. He may not be Force sensitive, but his abilities rival those of a Jedi Knight.

Homeworld: Kalee

Species: Kaleesh

Gender: Male

Height: 7 feet tall (at full height)

Weapon: Lightsabers, blaster pistol, electrostaff

Affiliation: Separatist Alliance

Commander Cody checks in with Anakin Skywalker and
Obi-Wan Kenobi

General Grievous prepares for invasion

Commander Cody and Captain Rex

Battle droids attack

Grievous is not pleased

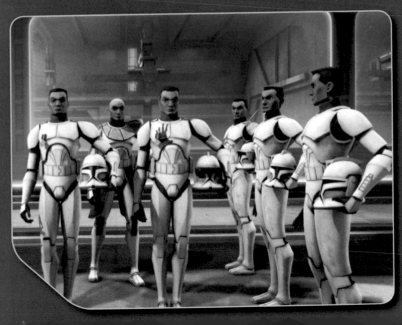

DOWNFALL OF A DROID

The Separatist frigate explodes

Anakin and R2-D2 prepare for their mission

Grievous is ready

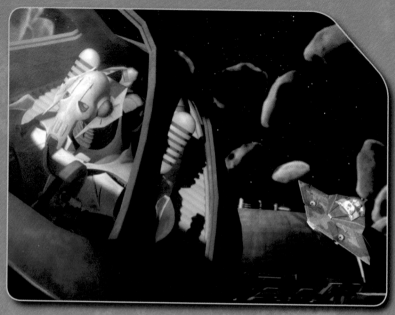

In pursuit of Grievous

The MagnaGuards capture R2-D2

Anakin in his starfighter

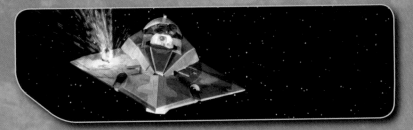

Anakin and R2-D2 take a hit

Ahsoka introduces R3-S6

Ahsoka is in trouble

R2-D2 confronts the evil R3-S6

R3-S6 attacks

But he's no match for R2-D2

Ahsoka is happy to have R2-D2 back

Grievous flees in defeat

LAIR OF GRIEVOUS

Nahdir Vebb and Kit Fisto arrive at Grievous's lair

Grievous attacks Kit

Nahdir and Kit battle Grievous

Grievous is cut down

A clone is caught

Meet Grievous's pet

Nahdir's last stand

Kit fights back

He had lost another chance at taking down Skywalker. But the Jedi's droid was on the way. Soon, the droid would be in his hands . . . along with all of the secrets it contained.

CHAPTER SEVEN

When the *Twilight* was safely out of Grievous's reach, Anakin resumed the search for the secret listening post. Ahsoka, R3, and Rex huddled over the scanner screens in the cockpit.

"We've searched their supply grids, sir," Rex informed Anakin. "There's nothing to indicate the presence of an enemy outpost."

Ahsoka held a headphone to her left ear. R3 had plugged his interface into a console next to her, scanning the area for stray sounds.

"Master, I'm receiving a strange transmission," Ahsoka said. "I can't seem to make it out, though."

Anakin hit a switch on the control panel, and a faint sound echoed in the cockpit.

"Boost the volume, Goldie," Ahsoka told R3.

The droid spun his interface, and the sound

faded instead of getting louder.

"No, you're losing it," Anakin said. He hit another switch, and the sound blared loudly over the speaker. It was the unmistakable signal of an astromech droid.

"Beep, beep, beep . . ."

"That's Artoo!" Anakin said.

"That doesn't sound like Artoo," Ahsoka said skeptically.

But Anakin was certain. "It's him. I could never forget that voice. Trace it, Rex!"

"Sir!" Rex replied. He turned to a work panel on the console.

"Master, our orders were to find the Separatist listening post," Ahsoka reminded him.

"Perhaps Artoo is at the listening post. Did you consider that?" Anakin asked.

Rex looked up from his screen. "We have a lock on the droid's location, sir."

Excited, Anakin sat down in the pilot's chair. "Prepare to jump to these coordinates."

Rex nodded. "Sir!"

Anakin gazed out through the viewport at the starry sky.

"Hold on, Artoo, old buddy. We're coming."

Anakin turned the *Twilight* around, and the ship jumped into hyperspace.

Gha Nachkt's scavenger ship, the *Vulture's Claw*, cruised through space toward the planet Ruusan. A cluster of moons hung in the planet's orbit.

As Gha Nachkt steered the ship, he spoke to a hologram of General Grievous on his control grid.

"I'm entering your orbit now, General. I will be at the station shortly," the reptilian creature said. His wide mouth twisted into a greedy grin. "And General, I prefer to get my reward in cash."

Grievous replied with an angry growl. Gha Nachkt turned off the holoprojector.

In the corner of the room, R2 was once again trying to get a message to Anakin. He had cut a hole into the wall panel and plugged into a computer port he'd found behind it. He nervously sent out a message through the ship's own transmitter dish.

But Gha Nachkt quickly realized something was wrong. He heard the signal from his console. When he went to switch it off on his control panel, the switch wouldn't work.

"What is going on here?" he asked angrily. He turned to his ship's computer. "Ro-Zee, what's the matter with you?"

Then Gha Nachkt realized what was happening. He spun around and scowled at R2.

"You'd better be worth all this trouble, you sneaky little scrap pile," he said. He marched to the cell and jabbed R2 with an electrified overload prod.

"*Beep!*" R2 cried out as he felt the electric jolt.

Gha Nachkt just laughed. Soon, he would be rich. And the droid would not be his problem anymore.

The *Vulture's Claw* reached the Separatists' secret base. Skytop Station hung high in the upper atmosphere of one of Ruusan's moons, hidden in the clouds. Gha Nachkt landed the ship and then hustled R2 toward the station's decoding room, where he was told he would find General Grievous.

R2 spun his domed head from left to right to see what he could learn. Six Aqualish technicians sat at holo-stations, decoding Republic messages. The Aqualish were fairly common throughout the galaxy. They were humanoid, but with spiderlike heads. Their faces were lined with coarse hair. Each Aqualish had two large, bulging eyes with two smaller eyes underneath. Distinctive downward-facing tusks covered their small mouths.

Gha Nachkt gave R2 another prod. "Keep

moving, grease pot."

One of the Aqualish turned to R2 and hissed as he walked by. R2 responded with a rude *pfftthhh*!

Suddenly, R2 found himself face-to-face with General Grievous. He beeped nervously.

"This is the droid those Jedi came looking for, General," Gha Nachkt said.

General Grievous bent down toward R2. "What secrets do you carry, my little friend?" he asked, his voice menacing.

"*Beep!*" R2 said angrily.

Grievous chuckled. "So defiant! No need to fear, we're all droids here." He turned to Gha Nachkt. "Rip this runt apart and find out everything he knows!"

R2 quickly backed up, running over Gha Nachkt's foot. The Trandoshan grunted. "Right away, General."

Zap! He prodded R2 once more, leading him to the back of the room. The droid beeped in alarm. A sinister-looking machine waited for him.

It was a droid disassembling rack!

CHAPTER EIGHT

The *Twilight* zoomed out of hyperspace and swung toward the cloud-covered moons of Ruusan. A clone pilot steered the ship while Rex studied a map of the planetary system on a console. Anakin and Ahsoka peered over Rex's shoulder.

"Sir, the last transmission came from that moon's upper atmosphere, directly ahead," Rex reported.

Suddenly, an image of a battlesphere appeared on Rex's scanner.

"That's a Separatist battlesphere!" Anakin cried.

"I'm picking up a lot of encrypted chatter," Ahsoka said.

"Contact Obi-Wan," Anakin instructed. He turned to R3. "Scramble secret code set 1-4-7-7. I don't want that station to pick this up."

R3 plugged his interface into the communication

console. A hologram of Obi-Wan appeared before them.

"Anakin?" Obi-Wan asked.

"We believe we've found your Separatist listening post," Anakin told him.

"Excellent work!" Obi-Wan said. "Back off and wait. I'll send two main line cruisers to help you destroy it."

"But Artoo . . ." Ahsoka began, worried.

"We believe Artoo is onboard," Anakin explained. "He's the one that led us here."

Obi-Wan frowned. "Hmmm. This complicates things. You must sneak aboard that station and destroy it before they crack Artoo's memory banks."

Anakin looked unhappy. He wanted to rescue R2, not destroy him.

"I know you're fond of that droid, but he's fallen into enemy hands," Obi-Wan pointed out.

"I could rescue him," Anakin said.

"No, this is not a rescue mission!" Obi-Wan interrupted.

His hologram disappeared. Anakin turned to the clone pilot.

"Keep jamming their scanners. If they spot us, we're dead."

Anakin stared at the giant battlesphere on the scanner. R2 was there somewhere. He had his orders from Obi-Wan, but Anakin knew what he had to do. He would destroy the station and save R2 at the same time.

Anakin quickly instructed the crew on his plan. They were all gathered in the hold of the ship, where Anakin's starfighter was stashed. Rex and four clone troopers readied their blasters for battle. Anakin loaded a backpack with thermal detonators and strapped it to his back.

Ahsoka strapped a harness strap to R3. Rex eyed her curiously.

"You're bringing the droid?" he asked.

"We'll need Goldie to open secured hatches and access the station's computer for us," Ahsoka explained. "Oh, and Rex, *you* get to carry him."

"Well, that's just great," Rex muttered.

The *Twilight* soared above the clouds, hovering above the listening station. The rear door hissed open. Ahsoka looked down at the swirling clouds and grinned.

"Follow me, boys!" she yelled as she jumped out of the ship.

Ahsoka spread her arms wide as she plummeted

down toward the station. Above her, Anakin, the four clone troopers, and Rex, R3 strapped to his chest, followed.

Soon the clouds parted, and the hull of the listening post came into view. Ahsoka and the others activated their rocket packs. They slowed down and then landed on the hull. Rex struggled with the weight of the heavy droid and nearly toppled over. The other clone troopers chuckled.

"Next time, you're lugging this astromech around," Rex grumbled.

Anakin ignited his lightsaber and cut a hole into the hull. Ahsoka cut the harness straps off of R3, and they all entered the secret post.

Two battle droids stood guard at the end of the corridor in front of them.

"All this moisture is corroding my servo-motors," one of the droids complained.

"Go up to level eight and get your head adjusted. It feels great," the other suggested.

"That sounds gr—" Before the battle droid could finish his sentence, one of the clone troopers snuck up on him and twisted off his head. The other droid turned.

"Hey!" the battle droid cried.

Rex blasted it to pieces before it could react. He motioned to Anakin and Ahsoka that all was clear. They all made their way down the corridor and stopped in front of a computer access panel.

"All right, Stubby. Get to work," Anakin instructed R3.

The droid plugged in, and his interface began to spin. A hologram of Skytop Station appeared in front of them. Captain Rex pointed to their current position, right in the center of the sphere.

"We're here," he said. "The reactors are thirty levels below us."

"Ahsoka, you take the squad and blow up those reactors," Anakin said. "Gravity will do the rest. We'll meet in the landing bay."

He handed Ahsoka the backpack full of thermal detonators. Ahsoka raised an eyebrow and smiled.

"Where are you going?" she asked.

"I'm just gonna have a little look around," Anakin replied innocently.

He ran off down the corridor. Ahsoka strapped on the pack of explosives.

"I hope you find Artoo in one piece," she called after him.

Anakin shook his head. "Get going, Snips!"

CHAPTER NINE

Ahsoka turned to Rex and the clone troopers.

"Looks like it's up to us to complete the mission. As usual," she said.

They headed off down the opposite end of the corridor. Ahsoka didn't notice, but R3 hung back. He ducked into an alcove and extended his dish antennae. A small hologram of General Grievous projected into the air in front of him.

"*Beep, beep, beep!*" R3 reported.

"The Jedi are here? Delay them until I arrive!" General Grievous ordered.

"Goldie, where are you!" Ahsoka called out.

R3 quickly folded up his antennae, not wanting to get caught. He rolled out of his hiding place and bumped into Ahsoka.

"What are you doing back there? Come on!" she

urged.

R3 rolled ahead. Ahsoka was puzzled. The droid was acting stranger than usual. But she couldn't worry about that now.

She had a station to blow up.

In the station's decoding room, Grievous barked an order to an Aqualish technician.

"Sound the alarm!"

The technician bowed and hurried away.

Nearby, R2 was strapped to the droid disassembling rack. His metal body had been opened wide, and wires and cables were attached to his inner workings. The droid's dome-shaped head had been removed. Those wires led to a control panel manned by Gha Nachkt.

The Trandoshan pressed a button on the panel, and R2 beeped out in alarm. His holoprojector activated, and an amazing display appeared above him. It showed blueprints, diagrams, star charts, and other documents detailing the Republic's battle plans.

Gha Nachkt's eyes widened. "This is . . . this is . . . General Grievous!"

The general stomped over. "What is it?"

Gha Nachkt nodded toward the slide show of

secrets being projected from R2.

"It appears this droid's mission memory has never been erased," he explained. "It contains every Republic formation and strategy they have!"

"Good work," Grievous said. "You certainly earned your fee this time."

"*More* than my fee," Gha Nachkt said greedily. "This droid is worth more, I get paid more. I suggest . . ."

Before the scavenger could even finish his sentence, Grievous had zapped him with a droid blaster, sending him flying back against a bulkhead.

The general gave an evil chuckle. "*There's* your bonus."

He moved closer to R2. "Now we will transfer all your secrets to me."

R2 was in no shape to fight back. He tried to beep, but could only manage a groggy whirring sound.

"Don't worry. I won't let anything happen to you," Grievous said.

Suddenly, a loud alarm began to blare throughout the station. Four MagnaGuards swept into the room, surrounding Grievous. The general's elite force of droid bodyguards looked much more menacing than regular battle droids. Each one wielded a double-ended staff that gave off a powerful electric charge on each end.

"Republic troops have infiltrated the base," Grievous informed them. "Keep this droid secured."

"Yes, sir," one of the MagnaGuards replied. They flanked R2.

Satisfied that R2 and his secrets would be safe, General Grievous stormed out of the decoding room.

"I will deal with the Jedi myself!"

CHAPTER TEN

Ahsoka and Rex quickly made their way to the generator room.

"We found the reactor room, sir," Rex told Anakin over the comlink. "The alarm triggered another security door. It has a ray shield on it."

Ahsoka looked over the door's glowing shield. "This could take a while to bypass."

"Good luck with that," Anakin replied. "I'm off to find Artoo."

Ahsoka nodded to R3. "Go ahead, Goldie. Make me proud."

R3 plugged into the door's electro lock panel and went to work.

"This'll be good," Rex said.

The four clone troopers stood guard while R3 tried to open the door. The sound of approaching super battle droids echoed down the corridor. The troopers raised their weapons.

"Those droids are getting close, sir," Rex said worriedly. "You think Arthree is going to open up that door anytime soon?"

"He's working on it," Ahsoka said. "Patience, Captain."

Now the sounds of metal footsteps were coming from another direction. They were about to be attacked from all sides! The troopers repositioned themselves so that two guards blocked each path.

"*I* can always hot-wire it, sir," suggested one of the troopers, a clone named Denal.

Ahsoka shot an annoyed glance at the clone. But he had a point. R3 was taking a long time.

"Hurry up, Goldie," she said urgently.

R3 beeped and spun his interface, but the shield still held. Then a squad of battle droids appeared at the end of the hall.

"I think we've run out of time," Rex said.

"Blast 'em!" yelled the droid commander.

The droids opened fire, blasting the clone troopers with bright red flashes from their laser weapons. The clones pressed against the walls and shot back. Then lasers streaked in from the other direction. Ahsoka ignited her lightsaber and charged at the droids. She expertly deflected the blasts aimed at R3 and Rex.

Suddenly, *another* door slammed down over the security door. R3 wasn't getting anything open—he was just making it worse! Rex glared at Ahsoka, who smiled sheepishly back at him. But there was no time to scold R3.

Four super battle droids were closing in on them. These bulkier, stronger droids had heavy chest plates and built-in double-laser cannons. They fired on Ahsoka and the clones.

"Rex, droid poppers, now!" Ahsoka yelled.

"Droid poppers!" Rex called out.

The troopers pulled EMP grenades from their belts and rolled them toward the super battle droids. The droids were powerful, but not very skilled. They tried to fire at the rolling grenades, but missed completely.

As the grenades stopped in front of the super battle droids, they popped up into the air and then let out a burst of EMP energy. The sudden energy burst fried the circuits of the super battle droids, which then crumbled to the ground.

Another grenade rolled toward the battle droids. One picked it up and looked at it curiously.

Pop! The EMP grenade exploded, frying the battle droids, too.

The droid attack was over. R3 finally had the door to the generator room opened. Ahsoka and the clones stepped inside, ready to place the charges.

Instead, they found General Grievous.

"They sent a child to destroy my station? The Republic must be running out of Jedi," he sneered.

"You must be General Grievous," Ahsoka said.

The general laughed and fell into a coughing fit.

"He's just another tinny, boys," Ahsoka said bravely. "Let's scrap him like the rest!"

She ignited her lightsaber and charged toward Grievous. The shaft of green light clashed with Grievous's blue lightsaber. The impact sent Ahsoka falling backward.

The air sizzled with purple fire as the clone troopers fired on Grievous with their blasters. Roaring, the general deflected the blasts with his lightsaber. The blasts slammed back at one of the clone troopers, who screamed and fell.

Grievous charged toward them, taking down two more clone troopers with swift moves of his lightsaber. He then kicked Rex into trooper Denal, sending them both flying. The general raised his lightsaber, ready to finish Rex.

Ahsoka jumped to her feet and ran forward, blocking the blow with her lightsaber.

"Sorry to interrupt your playtime, Grumpy, but wouldn't you prefer a challenge?" she quipped.

"That wouldn't be you," Grievous replied.

He swirled his cape aside, revealing a second lightsaber. He launched at Ahsoka. She realized that she was no match for the general and sprinted down the corridor.

R3 rolled down the corridor ahead of Ahsoka and beeped to get her attention. She followed the droid through a door. General Grievous caught up to them. He paused, talking into his comlink.

"All units stay on high alert," he said. "Watch out for a second Jedi loose in the station. And take the captured R2 unit to my ship."

Grievous entered the room that Ahsoka had escaped into. It was a storage area, cluttered with leftover gears, cogs, and other machine parts. There were narrow passageways between the junk, and deep shadows cast over the dim space.

"Where is that fight you promised me, youngling?" Grievous called out.

Ahsoka hid behind a console, trying to come up

with a plan. She raised her hand and used the Force to lift up a nearby tool. She sent it flying against a wall across the room. The trick fooled Grievous, just as she had hoped. He stomped off toward the noise.

Just then, Ahsoka's comlink began to flash. She pressed a button and heard Rex's voice.

"Ahsoka, it's me, Rex. There are only two of us left. Should we abort the mission?"

"No, complete the mission," Ahsoka whispered. "Set the charges and rendezvous at the landing bay."

"But, sir!" Rex protested.

"That's an order, Rex. I'll keep the general busy. Ahsoka out."

She quickly shut off the comlink. She could hear Grievous making his way through the storage room.

"Come here, child," he called out in a sinister voice. "I'm looking for you. So far, you have failed to impress me."

The voice was getting closer. Ahsoka moved from her hiding place to find a new one. To her surprise, she saw R3 rolling down the corridor, right out in the open!

"Goldie! Over here!" she hissed.

R3's head turned to face Ahsoka.

"BEEP!" Then his spotlight turned on, shining on

Ahsoka.

"Goldie, no!" she yelled.

Then a blue lightsaber blade slashed in front of her. Ahsoka tried to dodge it, but it grazed her wrist, cutting off her comlink.

"Ahsoka, we're in the reactor room," Rex announced over the comlink.

Grievous stepped on it, crushing the comlink with his metal foot.

"Your friends won't help you. You're stuck with me!"

Ahsoka ducked under a nearby console and dashed into the next passageway. Grievous turned and gave chase, chuckling.

There was no way the youngling could escape him now!

Back in the decoder room, the MagnaGuards carried R2 to a turbolift. The droid was still in pieces, but R2 had enough energy to let out a weak beep.

Anakin heard his friend and came running. "Artoo!" he cried out.

He ignited his lightsaber and charged across the room. The turbolift door opened, and three super battle droids came out! The MagnaGuards pushed past them to enter the lift, and the battle droids opened fire on Anakin.

"Hang on, Artoo!" Anakin yelled.

He deflected the laser cannon blasts with his lightsaber. At the same time, R2 reached out with his grasper arm and grabbed the doorframe of the turbolift, but one of the MagnaGuards wrenched it away. Anakin took care of the last super battle droid and ran to the turbolift, but he was too late. The door closed in front of him.

R2 let out a high-pitched wail as the turbolift zoomed through the station. The lift reached its destination and the doors opened. The MagnaGuards moved to take R2 out of the elevator.

Then a sizzling sound caused them to look up. A piece of the ceiling dropped down in front of them. Anakin swung down into the elevator and ignited his lightsaber.

"You have something that belongs to me," he said coolly.

The MagnaGuards dropped R2 in a heap and spun their electrostaffs. The two ends of the staff blazed with an electric charge. R2 ignited his rocket jets and flew into the clear. He quickly began to put himself back together.

The MagnaGuards surrounded Anakin. His lightsaber zipped through the air with swift accuracy. One of the guards' staffs clattered to the ground. Then Anakin chopped off the legs of the droid with one quick swipe.

He turned his attention to the other guard. With three quick slashes, he sliced off the droid's arms, and finished by cutting it down the center.

The first MagnaGuard reached for Anakin, but R2 rolled in and zapped the droid with his prod.

"Thanks, Artoo," Anakin said.

"*Beep!*" R2 replied. The beep sounded happy and tired at the same time.

R2's domed head wasn't on straight, so Anakin snapped it back into place. "It's great to see you, buddy. You don't look so good. You okay?"

"*Beep!*"

A crackle of static came over Anakin's comlink. He spoke into it.

"Rex, can you hear me? Arthree? Arthree, is that you? I've got Artoo. I'll meet you back at the landing bay."

R2 beeped questioningly at the mention of another mech droid.

"Arthree? Oh yeah, I had to get a replacement

droid," Anakin explained. "Sorry, Artoo."

Insulted, R2 turned his domed head away from Anakin and let out a jealous beep.

"It was Obi-Wan's idea," Anakin said. "We'll talk about this later."

R2 swung around to face Anakin again. With an obedient beep, he extended his dish antenna and signaled the *Twilight*.

"*Twilight*, this is Skywalker," Anakin said. "Rendezvous at the south landing bay immediately for evacuation."

"Acknowledged, General. I'm on my way," the clone pilot responded.

Anakin and R2 raced to the landing bay.

CHAPTER ELEVEN

Ahsoka hid under an old piece of equipment, hoping that Grievous wouldn't find her. Then she heard the general's voice.

"Arthree, what have you to report?"

R3 responded with a series of beeps. Ahsoka was shocked. The gold mech droid was a traitor!

"That stubby little backstabber," she muttered.

"So Skywalker has come for his R2 unit?" Grievous said. "Heh-heh. Go and make sure they do not escape."

"*Beep!*" R3 replied. Then he rolled toward the exit. Ahsoka's eyes narrowed in anger.

She had to find a way to warn Anakin.

Anakin and R2 entered the landing bay to see the *Twilight* set down in front of them.

"Great, there's our ship. But where's everyone else?" Anakin wondered.

The *Twilight*'s clone pilot walked out of the ship and saluted Anakin.

"Sir!"

Behind them, the turbolift doors opened and R3 rolled out.

"Hey, Stubby, where's Ahsoka?" Anakin asked.

R3 rolled right past Anakin, ignoring him. He passed R2, giving off a rude beep. He stopped at a computer port on the wall and plugged in.

"General Skywalker!"

Anakin turned to see Rex and trooper Denal stagger into the landing bay through a side entrance.

"Explosives are in place, sir. Objective completed," Rex reported.

"Where's Ahsoka?" Anakin asked.

"She engaged General Grievous," Rex replied.

Anakin was alarmed. "Alone?" Grievous was much more skilled in combat than Ahsoka, even if he was a wheezing heap of scrap metal.

"She distracted him while we completed the mission," Rex explained. He could clearly see how unhappy Anakin was. "It was on her orders, sir. The droid was with her."

"We gotta find her!" Anakin cried. "Stubby, locate Ahsoka!"

R3 ignored Anakin's command.

"I can take you to her, sir," Rex offered. He rushed back to the side entrance, but the door swiftly closed shut. Then the huge hangar door slammed down, trapping the *Twilight* inside the landing bay.

Anakin turned to R3. "What's the matter with you? Are you trying to get us killed?"

R3 spun his interface in the computer port. Anakin heard a sound from above. He looked up to see three vulture droids drop down from the ceiling. The fighters lowered their legs and marched toward Anakin and his crew.

"I've got a bad feeling about this, sir," Rex said.

The truth suddenly hit Anakin. "That double-crossing droid is a spy!"

A whirring sound filled the bay as the vulture droids powered up to fire. Anakin, Rex, and the clone troopers ran for cover behind a large metal support beam. The clones fired laser blasts at the approaching droids. Anakin deflected the bolts with his lightsaber.

"Captain, trigger the explosives in the generator!" Anakin ordered.

"But sir, we're still in the station," Rex said warily.

"Just let me worry about the details," Anakin replied.

"Sir, yes, sir!" Rex said.

He picked up the detonator and put his finger on the button.

Ahsoka gripped her lightsaber tightly. She could hear the general's footsteps as he came closer and closer. She couldn't hide forever, she knew.

The footsteps stopped suddenly. Ahsoka paused. What was Grievous up to? She stepped out of her hiding place tentatively, holding her breath.

The corridor was empty. She breathed a sigh of relief.

Then a metal hand reached down from the ceiling and grabbed her by the throat! Grievous stood upside down on the ceiling.

Ahsoka tried to raise her lightsaber, but Grievous knocked it from her hands. It skidded across the floor and disappeared into the shadows.

The general walked across the ceiling and down the wall like some kind of insect, still holding Ahsoka by the throat. She kicked fiercely, trying to break away from the powerful droid claw.

Grievous walked to her lightsaber and picked it

up. "Another lightsaber to add to my collection."

He ignited it and held it in front of her face.

"My spy droid, Arthree, has trapped your precious Master," he said. "When I've finished you, he's next."

"You're wrong," Ahsoka said. "He's gone by now, and he's gonna blow up your precious station."

"Not this time," Grievous said.

But he had barely finished his sentence when a loud *BOOM!* rocked the listening station. The floor of the storage room lurched, and Grievous lost his grip on Ahsoka's right hand for one second. Ahsoka quickly grabbed her lightsaber from his claws and slashed at Grievous's other hand, severing it from his arm and leaving only a mechanical stump.

Ahsoka ran across the floor, which was now on a slant thanks to the explosion. She jumped up into a ceiling vent and disappeared before Grievous could grab her again. Grievous slashed at the ceiling duct with his lightsaber in fury, but Ahsoka was already gone.

The general roared in anger and frustration.

He was beaten—by a youngling!

CHAPTER TWELVE

BOOM!

Another explosion rocked the station. R2 and R3 skidded across the floor of the ship's hangar. Piles of loose equipment and cargo containers crashed down around them. R2 slammed into a metal beam. He let out a dazed beep as he spun his dome to see Anakin taking cover behind the metal beam.

"Artoo, I need you to get the hangar door open!" Anakin said.

"*Beep?*" R2 replied.

"See if there are any controls on the outer platform!" Anakin instructed. He pointed to a small door across the hangar—a droid access hatch.

R2 quickly rolled across the floor and went through the hatch. He could see a control console on the outer platform, just as Anakin had guessed. The station lurched as another explosion rippled through it, and R2 tried to steady himself. He rolled to the hangar door control socket and got ready to plug in.

Slam! Just then, R3 rolled up and rammed into him from behind.

"*Wheeeeeeeee . . .*" R2 squealed as the force of the attack pushed him away from the control socket.

R2 quickly wheeled around and charged at R3.

The gold droid extended two clasper arms from his body. They reached out to grab R2. But R2 countered with a jolt of blue electricity from his eye. There was a sizzling sound as the jolt hit R3, and then the mech droid went dark.

Overhead, a Separatist fighter emerged from a hidden hangar in the station and sped away. It was General Grievous. Below him, the damaged listening station was beginning a slow plummet to the moon's surface.

It would take a miracle for the Jedi to escape this disaster.

Back in the hangar bay, Ahsoka swung down from the ceiling vent. Anakin, Rex, and Denal were exchanging blaster fire with a trio of vulture droids and a group of super battle droids.

Thinking quickly, Ahsoka dropped from the vent

and landed on top of the nearest vulture droid. She stabbed it in the head with her lightsaber. It wobbled for a moment and then collapsed. She jumped off of it before it hit the floor.

Another vulture droid turned to Ahsoka. Anakin somersaulted underneath it and stabbed it from below. Then he quickly rolled out of the way as it crumpled into a metal heap.

Rex and Denal blasted away at the super battle droids as the last vulture droid charged at Anakin and Ahsoka. They took cover behind a large metal beam.

"So, what'd I miss?" Ahsoka asked.

"Oh, the usual," Anakin replied.

A blast of laser fire zoomed toward them, and Ahsoka deflected it with her lightsaber.

"It was foolish of you to take on Grievous by yourself," Anakin scolded her.

Ahsoka shrugged. "Well, I was leading the mission, and it seemed like a good idea at the time."

"Did he tell you that your stubby little gold droid pal works for him?" Anakin asked.

Ahsoka cringed. "He might have mentioned it. I guess we were all fooled."

Anakin gave Ahsoka a look that said *I told you*

so. But they had more important things to worry about right now. That last vulture droid had them cornered.

"General Skywalker, there are fuel cells over here!" Captain Rex called out.

Anakin nodded. "Get ready, Rex!"

Anakin used the Force to lift up the fuel tank and hurl it right at the vulture droid. Just before it hit, Rex zapped it with his blaster.

BOOM! The tank exploded in a ball of fire, destroying the vulture droid and the battle droids behind it.

Just at that moment, R2 plugged into the console and opened the hangar door. Now the *Twilight* could make its escape. Anakin, Ahsoka, Rex, and Denal ran for the ship.

"Artoo did it!" Ahsoka cried as the floor tilted underneath them.

"Of course he did!" Anakin said. "Now let's get out of here!"

As they ran into the ship, Anakin scanned the platform for R2.

"Where are you, Artoo?" he wondered.

Back on the outer platform, R3 was recharged and ready to fight once more. Before R2 could unplug from the console, R3 slammed into the droid again.

They couldn't wait for R2. In seconds, the listening station would collide with the surface of the moon. Ahsoka revved up the ship and piloted it through the hangar door.

As the *Twilight* sped away, Anakin's starfighter dropped out of the bottom of the freighter.

"Where is General Skywalker going?" Rex asked.

Ahsoka knew. "He's going after Artoo."

Anakin put his fighter in a sharp dive, trying to keep up with the plummeting listening post.

A small fire blazed on the outer hangar platform, lighting up the battle between the two droids. R3 charged at R2, trying to zap him with his prod. R2 quickly dodged, squirting oil at R3. The gold droid slipped and slid backward to the platform rail.

R3 quickly shot out a grappler cable and latched onto R2. If he was going to fall, he wanted to take R2 with him.

But R2 had other ideas. He extended his spinning saw blade and cut through the cable. R3 tumbled backward over the rail and crashed onto the moon below. A chunk of the station fell right on top of him. *Ka-blam!*

"*Beep! Beep!*" R2 celebrated his victory. Then

he realized the station was about to crash. He gave a worried beep. Would it be his last?

Suddenly, through the clouds, Anakin's fighter dove in. He expertly piloted the craft next to the falling station.

"Come on, Artoo."

R2 rolled off the edge of the platform and dropped right into the astromech socket in the fighter. Anakin sped away just as the station slammed into the rocky surface of the moon, exploding in a cloud of fire and smoke.

Back on the *Twilight*, Ahsoka made some repairs to R2, while the droid applied some makeshift bandages to Anakin with his clasper arm. Obi-Wan watched the scene via hologram, and he wasn't happy.

"So let me get this straight, Anakin. You risked the mission, all your men, even your Padawan . . . to save a droid?"

"Artoo found the listening post and he saved our lives," Anakin pointed out. "We couldn't just leave him there, Obi-Wan."

Obi-Wan shook his head. "Anakin . . . one day. One day, Anakin. One day . . ."

Obi-Wan ended his transmission. There was

nothing more to say. Anakin would always do whatever he wanted.

Ahsoka looked at Obi-Wan. "I'm glad we got Artoo back, Master, but Obi-Wan does have a point."

"Ahsoka, I knew you would complete the mission," Anakin said, flattering her. "Besides, Artoo is more than a droid. He's a friend."

"*Beep!*" R2 agreed happily.

Lair of Grievous

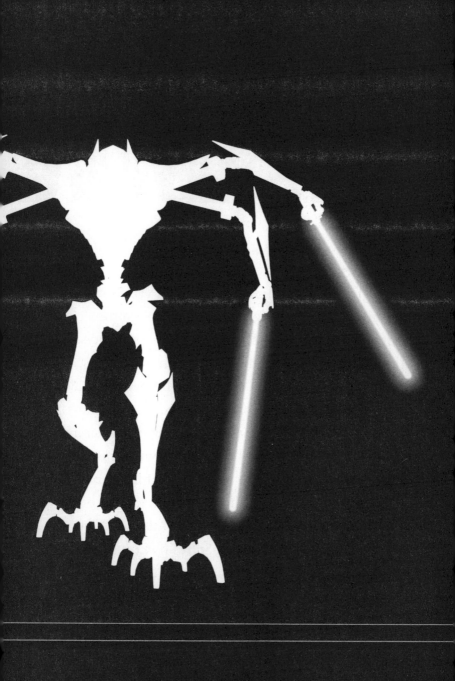

CHAPTER ONE

"Grievous is going to pay for this . . . I *will* destroy him."

Those words echoed through Kit Fisto's mind as his Delta-7B starfighter ripped through the atmosphere of Coruscant. With its massive cityscape that covered most of the planet's surface, Coruscant stood in stark contrast to his own homeworld. Glee Anselm was a peaceful and secluded planet located in the Mid Rim. Covered almost entirely by water and swamps, it was about as different from Coruscant as a planet could be. However, Kit felt at home on both worlds. One was where he was born, and the other was where he stood as a member of the Jedi Council.

As the glistening City of Spires of Coruscant began to rise on the horizon, Kit became more contemplative. Usually this sight would bring a slight smile to the Nautolan's face, but not on this day. He had some very troubling news to deliver to the Council, and it weighed heavily on him.

Kit made his way to the Jedi Temple. For thousands of years, the Temple had been home to the Jedi Order. It was a massive structure that stood over half a mile tall and overlooked all of Galactic City. The Temple was built around an ancient Force nexus that was located in a natural mountain known as the Sacred Spire. The Jedi Temple had five spires built on top: one tall temple spire surrounded by four smaller ones. These spires symbolized a Jedi's climb to enlightenment. Each of the four spires crowned a different quarter of the Temple, and each of these quarters was specialized for a variety of different purposes. The First Knowledge quarter was the most important in the training of younglings, while the High Council quarter was where the Jedi Council was located. The area around the Reassignment tower was dedicated to the public entrance, while the Reconciliation quarter had many gardens.

Kit entered the large, sunlit High Council chamber. Jedi Masters Yoda and Mace Windu sat in two of the twelve seats that formed a circle around the room. Mace Windu was an imposing figure. His dark and guarded stare rarely allowed any emotion to escape. Even with Kit's Nautolan head tresses, the fourteen tendrils that covered his head and allowed him to sense the emotional states of others, he could not read the Jedi Master's feelings.

"And what of your former Padawan?" Master Windu asked as he noticed the second lightsaber hanging from Kit's waist.

Yes, Kit thought as he looked down at his waist, *my former Padawan . . .*

They had been dispatched by the Jedi Council to track down Viceroy Nute Gunray, the Nemoidian head of the Trade Federation and a high-ranking member of the Separatist Alliance. The Separatists were the enemy of the Galactic Republic and of the Jedi. They were led by the Sith Lord Count Dooku, who was once a Jedi Master before falling to the dark side.

Nute Gunray had been captured by the Republic and was on his way to Coruscant to stand trial for the crimes that he had committed against the Republic when Dooku's agents had helped him escape from custody and flee in a stolen Republic frigate.

Following the homing signal of the stolen frigate,

Kit Fisto had been able to track Gunray to a small crater-scarred world in the Vassek system. As Kit pulled his starfighter out of hyperspace, a blinking dot appeared on his display. It was Gunray.

"Beep! Beep!" His astromech droid, R6-H5, beeped wildly with concern.

"I know that we're in the middle of nowhere, Arsix," the Jedi called to his droid. "But that's the Republic beacon we're looking for. Contact the Outer Rim command."

Moments later, a hologram appeared before him in the cockpit of the starfighter. It was Jedi Master Luminara Unduli and the Padawan, Ahsoka Tano.

"Master Luminara," Kit announced. "I have tracked the location of our stolen ship."

"So has your old Padawan, Nahdar Vebb," the Mirialan Jedi Master added. "He's already on the surface."

"It'll be great to see Nahdar again," Kit said. It had been a while since the struggles of the war had separated him and his old friend.

"I'll transmit the coordinates for the rendezvous point," Ahsoka added. "And Master Fisto . . . sorry we lost that slimy double-dealer."

"Don't worry, Ahsoka," Kit replied while offering

the young Padawan a reassuring wink. "We'll catch Gunray yet."

"Good hunting," replied Ahsoka with a smile as the hologram faded away.

The third moon of Vassek was a rocky, moss-covered world with giant canyons of jagged rock and an ominous, ever-present layer of fog.

Kit's starfighter ripped through the hazy sky and made a landing on a narrow rocky ledge that overlooked a massive gorge.

Once safely on the ground, R6 spun his dome around and beeped nervously. *Beep! Beep!*

"Well, I can't see anything either," Kit replied to his trusty droid. "You'll be fine, Arsix. Just keep a lookout, okay?"

Kit leaped from his starfighter and made his way through the fog. After a few steps, he came across a Republic attack shuttle that had also landed on the ledge. A hooded figure stood flanked by a group of clone troopers.

The cloaked figure stepped forward and removed his hood to reveal the large eyes and fishlike domed head of a Mon Calamari. With a bow, he greeted Kit Fisto.

"Nahdar!" Kit said as he flashed a pleased smile. "Congratulations on passing the trials. I'm sorry that the war prevented me from seeing your training to the end."

It was Jedi tradition for a Master to stay with his pupil and continue their training until the teacher felt that the Padawan was ready to be brought before the Jedi High Council for the trials of Knighthood. These trials were presented to any Padawan that the Council deemed worthy of becoming a Jedi Knight. The four trials were physically difficult and emotionally strenuous. The Council had to make sure that the young Jedi were able to control both their powers and their feelings before they were allowed to become Jedi Knights.

"You were missed, Master," Nahdar replied respectfully. "It is, however, an honor to serve beside you as a Jedi Knight."

One of the clones, Commander Fil, addressed Kit. "General, we've pinpointed the tracking beacon's location." Fil looked at a small handheld scanner. He paused for a moment and then gestured off into the fog. "It's at the south end of the gorge."

Kit turned to where the clone was pointing. The fog was so thick that he couldn't even see five feet in front of him. He smiled and turned to Fil. "Let's have a look."

"Allow *me* to show the way," Nahdar said as he raised his arms in the air.

The power of the Force swelled in the Mon Calamari as the fog covering opened up and revealed a structure on the gorge's far side. It was a creepy, fog-shrouded fortress made of stone and carved right into the jagged cliff.

"Charming." Kit smiled. "Let's not keep the Viceroy waiting."

Kit and Nahdar took off toward the fortress.

Commander Fil turned to his men. "Niner, Bel," he ordered. "Look after the ships. The rest of you, you're with me."

Fil and three clones charged off after the Jedi. As they moved out of sight, the fog closed in around them, appearing to swallow them up.

R6 beeped woefully as Kit moved out of sight.

CHAPTER TWO

The team, led by Kit, stealthily approached the fortress. It was a massive structure with no doors or windows, just mammoth stone blocks.

"No guards, that's odd," Kit said as he examined the structure.

"The entrance looks sealed," Nahdar added.

Commander Fil reached for a thermal detonator on his belt. "Good thing we specialize in making entrances."

Not to be outdone, Nahdar pulled out his lightsaber. "This will make less noise."

"Patience, the both of you," Kit chided. "A second look usually pays off."

The Jedi Master continued to search the wall until he came across a section that was smooth and not covered in moss. It looked to Kit as if it had recently been scraped away.

"What is this?" Kit asked as he pressed the stone and activated a hidden trigger plate in the wall. All of a sudden, a massive block of stone rumbled aside, revealing a secret door. Kit looked back and smiled at Nahdar and the troopers.

Once through the secret door, Kit led Nahdar and the clones down a dark and narrow corridor. The winding hallway intersected with several other passages that either ended in closed doorways or stretched on seemingly forever into the darkness.

"Do you smell that?" one of the clone troopers asked.

"It doesn't smell like droids to me," a second trooper added. "And it's too dark to see anything."

The clones turned on their helmet lights and flooded the corridor with light. Kit smiled and made his way down the illuminated hallway. Nahdar and the clones were right behind him. Suddenly the elder Jedi stopped in his tracks.

"I sense there's something down here," Kit said.

The clone troopers looked around, but they couldn't hear anything except the eerie howl of the wind blowing through the vast corridors and tunnels.

"Scanners are negative, General," Commander Fil reported.

The two Jedi looked around. They knew that there was something out there. Their senses were stronger than any scanner. Suddenly, a monstrous growl echoed through the maze of corridors.

"Well, that was something," one of the clone troopers commented.

Kit swiftly moved around the corner and discovered an open doorway with light flooding out of it. As they moved closer, they heard a familiar voice.

"All droids stay on guard," Nute Gunray commanded. "Be ready for anything."

"Roger, roger," a battle droid replied.

With that, Kit gave Fil a hand signal and they all began to move cautiously through the door and up an ascending stairwell toward the source of the light. At the top of the stairs was a large, column-lined chamber that led to a panoramic window overlooking the foggy gorge. The window was armored with slats that allowed shafts of light to beam into the room.

A tall chair faced the window. Gunray wasn't visible, but he could be heard ordering about the five battle droids that were standing in front of the chair.

Kit and Nahdar entered the room. With silent precision, the clone troopers followed, darting in and out behind the pillars. The two Jedi walked straight down the center of the room.

"Uh, Viceroy, the Jedi are here," one of the battle droids called out.

"I know that they're near," Gunray hollered back. "Once those Jedi pick up my trail, they'll never leave me alone."

The droid paused nervously before adding, "They're right behind you."

"What? Where?" Gunray cried out. "Do something! Blast them!"

As the droids moved into position, the Jedi stopped their advancement and the four clones appeared from behind the columns.

One of the droids turned to one of the other droids and asked, "Have you ever killed a Jedi?"

"No, never," it replied.

"Me neither," the first one admitted.

The droids paused briefly to consider their situation before opening fire. Kit skillfully deflected a bolt back into one, destroying it.

Another of the droids was trapped between the four clones and the two Jedi. It was easily outnumbered.

"Don't even think about it, Republic dogs!" the droid ordered nervously as it shifted its blaster's aim from one clone to the next.

Less than a moment later, all the clones fired at once. The droid was blown to bits.

Nahdar charged at the two remaining droids and aggressively chopped through them. Then, using the Force, he pushed the remains across the room.

The young Jedi turned and faced his Master, who gave him a disapproving stare.

"I didn't forget to teach you restraint, did I, my old Padawan?" Kit asked. He was concerned about his former student's aggressive behavior.

"I'm sorry, Master, I got carried away," Nahdar replied. He knew that he was allowing his judgment to become clouded.

"Those who have power should restrain from using it," Kit added. The young Jedi Knight was not above his teachings.

As the two Jedi spoke, they moved toward the Viceroy's chair from either side.

"Lieutenant!" Gunray called out. "Did you get them?"

Kit reached for the chair, but Nahdar quickly raised his hand and used the Force to spin it around.

"No, but we have you, Viceroy!" the young Jedi called out.

"You have nothing, Jedi fools!" Gunray laughed as the chair spun around to reveal just a hologram of the Viceroy. "I welcome you to your doom!"

The hologram flickered briefly before fading away. On the chair sat a small, palm-sized tracking beacon—the same one Kit and Nahdar had been following.

"He knew we were coming," Nahdar said.

"I should have known Gunray wasn't here." Kit spoke as he attempted to surmise their situation. "At the first sight of us, he would have run off screaming like the coward that he is."

A second voice came from the chair. "I apologize for the deception, Master Jedi."

"Count Dooku," Kit said calmly as a hologram of the count appeared in the chair. "You have a great talent for unexpected appearances."

"It's a shame that you came so far for nothing," Dooku added. "While the Viceroy is unavailable for capture, allow me to offer you an alternative prize . . . if you're up to the challenge."

Before the Jedi could respond, the hologram faded and a small button on the chair began to blink.

"This has got to be a trap," one of the clone troopers said as the Jedi exchanged glances.

Kit looked at the button and smiled. "It looks as if Dooku is trying to catch someone, and we're the bait."

"But who has the trap been set to catch?" Nahdar looked at Kit as he leaned in and pressed the flashing button.

Instantly, a heavy door on the far wall shook open. Through the door, the Jedi could see a shadowy hallway. "Shall we find out?" the young Jedi added.

"This place looks like a shrine to some strange warrior," Kit said as he made his way down the hallway. The walls of the corridor were lined with three statues of a creature in various stages of transformation. The first was of an alien warrior. The second was of a robotically enhanced fighter. But the last one was the most frightening of all. The alien had been completely transformed into a monstrous cyborg.

The two Jedi paused in front of that third statue for a moment before Kit finally spoke. "This is the lair of General Grievous!"

Grievous's starfighter dropped out of hyperspace over the third moon of Vassek. He aimed his ship toward the cratered world and was beginning his descent when his console began to blink. With a growl, he hit the switch and a hologram of Count Dooku appeared.

"Yes, my Lord?" Grievous asked his Sith Master.

"General, the ongoing stalemate in the war has become unacceptable. There is concern that you have lost your focus. Lord Sidious demands more dramatic results. More dead Jedi."

"You expect victory over the Jedi," an irritated Grievous replied. "But all you give me to fight them are battle droids."

Back on the moon, the Jedi and the clones

continued to make their way deeper into Grievous's fortress.

"These must be trophies," a visibly upset Nahdar said as he stood in front of a case displaying dozens of lightsabers. "They've been taken from the Jedi that he's murdered. There are so many."

Kit was too preoccupied with uncovering Dooku's plan to console his friend. "But why would Dooku want to set a trap for his best general?" he asked. "It doesn't make sense."

Nahdar looked up from the trophy case. "Are we the bait? Or is Grievous the bait?"

"We must consider who this trap is *actually* for," Kit pondered.

A chime from Kit's comlink alerted him to an incoming message.

"General, your droid is detecting an incoming ship," clone trooper Niner announced. "It matches the description of General Grievous's fighter, and it's headed our way."

"Keep out of sight and stand by for further orders," Kit responded to the trooper.

Nahdar couldn't contain his excitement. "Capturing Grievous could turn the tide of the war!" he exclaimed.

"And if he doesn't know we're here," Commander Fil added, "then we could plan a nice little surprise for him."

"Don't underestimate Grievous," Kit warned. "We *will* need a plan."

Once inside his grim lair, Grievous bolted from a turbolift and made his way down a dark and ominous hallway.

"Guards? Guards!" he hollered, expecting his MagnaGuards to be waiting for him. Frustrated, he called to his pet. "Gor! Gor! Where are you?"

Irritated, he stomped down the corridor. Before he could react, Kit and two clones stepped out in front of him. Nahdar and the two other clones appeared from side passages and closed in behind him. Grievous was trapped.

"Welcome home, General," Kit said with a smile. "I'm afraid that I must request your surrender." The Jedi raised his green glowing lightsaber. "Cooperate, Grievous, and perhaps the Senate will be merciful."

The general growled, "It is you who will get no mercy!"

He immediately ignited his two lightsabers and swung them at the Jedi, but the walls of the corridor were too narrow for him to maneuver. The Jedi had chosen their battleground well. Kit and Nahdar moved in from both sides with their own attacks.

Splitting his two arms into four, Grievous pulled two more lightsabers from his cloak. He turned his body sideways so that he could fight the Jedi on either side of him with two lightsabers each. It took all that the two Jedi had to hold off Grievous's advances.

"Cables!" Kit called to the clone troopers on his side of the corridor.

Following his order, the two clones fired the ascension cables from the bottoms of their blasters into Grievous. Grappler darts attached to cables pierced his robotic leg.

Grievous swung a lightsaber and cut one of the cables, but Kit was able to prevent him from getting to the other. The two clones on Nahdar's side fired their cables and put two darts into the general's other leg.

The troopers dug in and yanked on their cables. They struggled to subdue Grievous, but he fought like a wild animal.

"Don't let him go!" Commander Fil ordered his men.

As the clone troopers worked to hold Grievous in

place, Grievous maniacally swung his lightsabers at the cables.

"Don't let him cut the lines!" Kit called out as he ducked below a wild attack by Grievous. Focusing, he swung his lightsaber and, with a precision blow, sliced Grievous's robotic legs off at the knees.

As he began to collapse to the floor, Grievous leaped up and grabbed on to one of the pipes on the ceiling. The clone troopers immediately yanked on the cables and pulled him to the ground. With his arms, Grievous began to drag himself down the corridor.

Nahdar moved in to block the general's escape. "Don't make me destroy you," he threatened.

As Kit gave his former student a concerned look, he noticed Grievous spin one of his lightsabers to engage Nahdar. Deftly, Kit lunged forward and knocked the lightsaber out of Grievous's hand.

With his free hand, Grievous grabbed at the cables attached to him and used his great strength to yank the clones toward him from both directions, knocking the Jedi off balance.

"Come and get me!" Grievous roared as he kicked Kit back into the clones. Nahdar seized the opportunity to finish Grievous off. He stepped forward with his lightsaber blazing, but Grievous grabbed a clone and pulled him in between himself and the Jedi.

Stunned, the young Jedi hesitated for an instant. Having created an opening, Grievous thrust the clone toward Nahdar, knocking back the Mon Calamari.

Dropping on all fours, Grievous skittered toward Commander Fil. The clones opened fire. A blast grazed off of Grievous's mask, but that was it. With insectlike agility, Grievous quickly made his way down the corridor and out of sight.

Kit got to his feet and raced after Grievous.

"Cut him off!" Nahdar ordered to the clones as he, Fil, and a clone headed off down one of the corridors. The remaining two clones raced down a different corridor after Kit.

Fil and Nahdar spotted Grievous as he raced by an intersection. Fil fired his blaster, but couldn't make contact. Elsewhere in the maze, Kit heard the blaster fire and charged in that direction. When he arrived, he found two dead clones on the ground; they were the ones that had taken off behind him. Grievous had to be close. Kit kept moving.

CHAPTER FOUR

Grievous skittered around a corner and looked back to make sure that no one was around. He pushed a series of tiles on a walled doorway and it unlocked a secret escape hatch. The doorway closed quickly behind him and the tiles popped back into place. There was no sign that the doorway had ever existed.

A moment later, the Jedi and the clones converged to find that Grievous had disappeared. Kit and Nahdar exchanged glances. The young Jedi was visibly frustrated by Grievous's escape.

"The clones got in the way! I could have taken him," Nahdar said angrily.

"Let's just take care of the wounded," Kit replied to his former student. He was worried that Nahdar was losing control of his emotions.

"Doctor! Where are you?" Grievous howled as he pulled himself through the hatch of a large domed chamber with a massive control panel in the center. With great effort, he pulled himself up. There was smoke pouring from his armor where he had taken blaster fire.

An A4-D surgical droid rolled into the chamber.

"Greetings, Master. Look what you've let the Jedi do to you!" the droid said. "What a walking scrap pile! What a mess! It's going to take me forever to get you back into decent shape."

Grievous turned with an impatient glare. The general was not pleased with A4-D.

"Don't be upset with me, Master," the droid replied, not fazed by Grievous's rage. "If you were a better fighter, we would not be having this conversation. Now, I'll go fetch some spare parts."

The droid turned and rolled away.

Six humanoid droids hung from recharge cables suspended from the chamber's domed ceiling. They were Grievous's deadly bodyguards, the MagnaGuards.

"What happened to my bodyguards?" Grievous called to the medical droid.

"They were remotely deactivated for recharge,"

A4-D replied. "I thought that you did it."

Grievous narrowed his eyes suspiciously as he moved to activate a button on the wall. The eyes of the six MagnaGuard droids illuminated the darkness. The recharge cables detached and the six guards dropped to stand around Grievous.

"Lock down the perimeter!" the general ordered as he moved to the surgical chair that was positioned before the central control console. Grievous activated one of the security view screens. An image of Kit and Nahdar appeared before Grievous. The two Jedi knelt beside the body of a fallen clone.

"Let me go after Grievous myself, Master," the younger Jedi pleaded.

"Patience, Nahdar," Kit cautioned. "You may no longer be a Padawan, but you are not ready to take on Grievous."

The Jedi Master pondered the situation. "It is time that we retreated," Kit said as he turned toward the direction that they had come.

Kit led Nahdar and the clone troopers back out of the maze. As the Jedi approached the lair's exit, a massive stone slab suddenly slammed shut in front of them. When they turned to find an alternate route out of the fortress, they could hear more stone doors closing. They were locked in.

Kit and Nahdar exchanged uneasy looks.

"I guess we're going to have to fight after all," Kit said.

"Green scout to watcher base," Commander Fil radioed to the clones that were guarding the ships. "Contact the fleet at Besteene. Inform them that we've engaged Grievous and require reinforcements."

A moment later, they heard a tremendous explosion over the comlink.

Kit flipped on his comlink and could only hear R6's frantic beeping.

"Get out of there, Arsix. Now!" Kit ordered.

CHAPTER FIVE

A hologram appeared in front of them in the corridor.

"You've run out of time," Grievous said.

"Why don't you come out, General? Show us some of that Separatist hospitality," Kit replied.

"Patience," Grievous laughed. "In the meantime, please experience all that my home has to offer. It has been prepared especially for uninvited guests like you."

The hologram faded from view and the sound of hydraulics and gears roared to life behind a stone door. Suddenly, several stone blocks dropped out from under them, revealing a fiery incinerator pit.

With lightning-fast reflexes, the two Jedi quickly leaped to the safety of the adjoining hall. The two clones tumbled down into the pit. Commander Fil spun in midair and aimed his blaster up toward the edge of the pit. He fired the ascension cable into the stone of the wall. The cable pulled tight and snapped him to a stop just above the flames of the incinerator. The commander looked down—his fellow clone was not so lucky.

Nahdar grabbed at the cable and worked to pull Fil from the pit. The slime-covered floor made it difficult for him to get good footing, and the more that he pulled on the cable, the more he slid toward the pit. Kit leaped to his side and together they pulled Fil out of the fire.

"General," Kit called to the robotic camera that was watching them, "I know that you're watching. We've seen the lower levels of your home. We're not impressed."

Grievous's laugh echoed through the darkness. "Good, Jedi. Good. You will provide some sport for me yet."

Deeper in the maze, a dark, slime-covered door opened and revealed a horrible, monstrous creature obscured by shadows. The beast moved into the light of the corridor and exposed its hideous form. The roggwart stood tall on two hind legs. Its clawed hands and tridentlike tail swung wildly as it let out a long, deep growl.

A4-D approached General Grievous with a tray of spare parts.

"Master, the armor patches are getting cold," it said. "And contrary to your belief, I do have other things to do."

"Proceed with my repairs!" Grievous replied angrily.

The medical droid activated a switch on Grievous's chair. Hydraulic pumps hissed as the chair pivoted and extended back like a surgical table.

A4-D looked Grievous over. "Sometimes I wonder why you submitted to these changes," it said, not really expecting an answer.

Grievous threw the medical droid an angry stare. "Improvements!!" he bellowed. "I submit to no one. I chose them. Now get on with it."

The medical droid turned away and activated the controls for the chair. Robotic arms extended from the bottom and began to work on Grievous. One pulled a grappler dart from the remains of one of his mechanical legs. A robotic claw grabbed his damaged arm, pulled it off, and replaced it with a brand-new one.

A small pair of claws grabbed at Grievous's damaged mask.

"There may be some discomfort," A4-D said.

Grievous let out a massive groan of pain as the mask pulled away with a crunch, revealing the horrific, scarred remains of his real face.

"Stand firm," Kit ordered at hearing the ghastly roar of the roggwart. "There might be worse things here than Grievous."

Suddenly the ferocious monster appeared in the corridor. The giant beast bounded toward them at surprising speed.

"It looks like you're right about that, sir," Fil replied as he steadied his blaster on the beast.

Kit slashed at the creature with his lightsaber, but the beast's tough, armored skin knocked his lightsaber to the ground. Kit ran to retrieve it as Commander Fil readied his blaster.

"Shoot it, Commander!" Nahdar called out.

Fil took aim and fired at the creature, but its rocky hide absorbed the blasts without harm.

Nahdar grabbed onto the creature as it passed and climbed up onto its back. The roggwart reared up and tossed the Jedi to the ground. With its long, pointed tail, it grabbed Fil and yanked him off of his feet. Nahdar tried to distract the beast by slashing at it, but once again he was knocked to the ground. Kit ignited his lightsaber and stabbed the creature, piercing its tough skin. The roggwart reared up angrily and smashed Commander Fil, still wrapped in its tail, against the ground.

The creature raised its tail to smash Fil a second time, but Nahdar moved in and slashed the beast's tail in half. Kit moved quickly and sliced off its front legs with a quick slash of his lightsaber.

The roggwart roared in pain, then collapsed to the ground. Kit finished the beast with a single strike.

Nahdar stood over the dead body of Commander Fil. "Grievous is going to pay for this. I *will* destroy him," he said with rage in his voice. The Jedi clutched his lightsaber tightly in his webbed hand.

Kit looked over at his former pupil. He could see the anger boiling in Nahdar's eyes. "I understand your pain," he said. "But you forget your teachings. Revenge is not the way."

Nahdar spun to face the elder Jedi. "But this is war," he said as he thrust his hand toward the fallen body of Commander Fil. "Strength prevails. The rules have changed."

"Perhaps you are the one who has changed . . ." Kit replied. He was worried that Nahdar's training had ended too soon, and that he had not spent enough time with his student. Perhaps Nahdar was not ready to be a Jedi Knight.

"Come now," Kit called to Nahdar. "We need to keep moving."

CHAPTER SIX

Grievous sat up in his surgical chair. His cold eyes flickered behind his new armor mask.

"Let's see if Gor is finished playing with the Jedi," Grievous said as he looked down at the monitors on his command console. Half of the security monitors were filled with nothing but static. There was no sign of the Jedi or the clones.

"Where are they?" he asked.

He then noticed a monitor that revealed his dead pet, Gor, lying on the ground. He roared in frustration.

A4-D approached and gestured to a blinking light on the console.

"Master," the droid said. "You have an incoming transmission from Count Dooku."

Grievous smashed a button on the console and a

hologram of Dooku appeared before him.

"General," Dooku taunted. "I understand the Jedi have infiltrated your lair."

Grievous narrowed his eyes and gave Dooku a hard stare.

"Your recent defeats at their hands have shaken my faith in your ability to lead the droid army," the count continued. "I'm sure that you understand my need to reassess your effectiveness."

"YOU!" General Grievous accused. "You deactivated my guards! You let the Jedi in here! So you could test me?!"

"I do hope you emerge victorious," Dooku replied. He appeared pleased by Grievous's rage. "It is time for you to prove yourself."

Before Dooku could say anything more, Grievous deactivated the hologram.

"All right, Count," he said as he rose from his chair. "I'll play your little game."

A4-D moved to block his exit. "In your condition," it warned, "you need your rest."

"I'll rest when the Jedi are dead," Grievous growled as he made his way out of the secret hatch to where his MagnaGuards stood waiting for him. From the shadows, two sets of eyes followed their moves.

The Jedi watched as Grievous hit a combination on the panels on the door, locking it shut.

After the general and his guards were out of sight, the two Jedi headed for the secret door.

"You were right, Master," Nahdar said. "That exit must lead to the control room."

Kit smiled at the young Jedi and triggered the tiles to open the secret hatch.

Inside the control room, A4-D was cleaning up the smashed control console when he saw the two Jedi on a security monitor entering the chamber.

"Oh, what do we have here? Unwanted guests," the droid said as he activated the PA system.

"Master," the droid spoke into the microphone. "The Jedi are about to enter the control room!"

Kit and Nahdar realized that they'd been spotted.

"Nahdar, inside. Hurry!" Kit called to the young Jedi as he moved through the intersection of the secret door.

"No, you go," Nahdar announced. "I will hold them off."

"There's no time to argue," Kit replied. He could sense the anger flowing through his former student.

"We just can't run," Nahdar said, clutching his lightsaber. "We must finish this."

"Nahdar, now!" Kit pleaded.

It was too late. The secret door to the control room slammed shut, trapping Kit inside the chamber and Nahdar out in the corridor.

"I've been waiting for this!" Nahdar announced with pleasure as he ignited his lightsaber and turned to face Grievous and his MagnaGuards.

"Nahdar!" Kit called from the other side of the door. The young Jedi was trapped and there was nothing Kit could do to help him.

Charging down the corridor, Nahdar attacked a pair of the MagnaGuards. With fierce lightsaber strokes, he overpowered and defeated both of them. Another MagnaGuard attacked, but Nahdar was up to the task. The young Jedi used a combination of Force-pushes and lightsaber strikes to disarm his opponent and destroy it.

"Greetings, young Jedi," Grievous taunted as he stalked out of the shadows.

Nahdar easily destroyed a fourth guard as he turned and stood face-to-face with General Grievous.

"And where is your Master?" Grievous asked while scanning the hallway for Kit.

"You will find out soon enough," Nahdar replied as he charged at the general.

Grievous ignited two of his lightsabers and locked blades with the young Jedi.

"You can't defeat us all," Nahdar added as Grievous knocked him back.

"Of course I can," Grievous laughed as he lunged forward. His lightsaber blades spun menacingly through the stale air.

Nahdar moved quickly and blocked the general's attack. He could feel his anger growing as he struggled to hold off Grievous's assault. His emotions were beginning to take over and he no longer felt at one with the Force.

CHAPTER SEVEN

Back in the control room, A4-D watched the fight on one of the security monitors.

"Get him, Master! Kill him!" it called out. Then it realized something. "Wait. Where's the other Jedi?"

It looked quickly over at a monitor and saw that Kit was coming up from behind.

"Oh no," the droid said as Kit swung his lightsaber and cut its head clean off. The Jedi rushed to the control panel to see if there was a way for him to save his friend. On one of the monitors he saw Nahdar fighting with Grievous.

Kit watched his fellow Jedi battle with the monstrous general. Nahdar had his lightsaber locked with Grievous's two lightsabers. It appeared to be a standoff, but then Grievous detached one of his other arms and reached around his back and produced a blaster from his cloak.

Nahdar looked down. His lightsaber was locked; there was nothing he could do to defend himself. Grievous fired the blaster and Nahdar fell to ground, dead.

"No!" Kit cried from the control room. He was helpless to do anything to protect his former Padawan.

Grievous leaned in over Nahdar's body and picked up the dead Jedi's lightsaber. Another trophy. The sight of it burned in Kit's stomach. He knew that he couldn't let his emotions get the best of him. That was not the Jedi way.

Grievous looked up at the security camera.

"I will kill you all!" he screamed. "Do you hear me, Jedi? Do you hear me?"

At the moment, Kit's comlink blinked. It was his astromech droid, R6. He had returned with the starfighter.

"Meet me at the south landing," Kit told R6. "I'll be right there."

"*Beep, beep*," R6 replied as Kit watched Grievous on the monitor.

"I'm coming for you next, Fisto!" Grievous screamed at a security camera.

Kit's eyes narrowed and he pushed a few buttons on the command console. Throughout the maze, all of Grievous's death traps activated.

"I'll be gone by the time you get here," he replied as he ignited his lightsaber and slashed the console down the center, destroying it.

Kit exited the control room and moved toward the edge of the landing platform to meet R6. As he waited for his droid, he sensed something. Before he could react, a lightsaber sliced at his feet.

It was Grievous. He was hanging from the stone ledge below Kit. His clawed feet were dug deep into the rock. The general quickly leaped up, black smoke pouring from his armor.

"Going somewhere?" Grievous asked as he landed on the platform. His four lightsabers illuminated the sky.

Kit flew out of the fog and engaged Grievous. The general spun his four lightsabers like propellers and drove Kit back.

Suddenly Kit somersaulted over Grievous's head. The general turned and slashed with his lightsabers, but Kit had vanished back into the fog.

The Jedi's lightsaber ignited behind Grievous, who pivoted on his axis and blocked Kit's blow.

"You might have been a proud warrior once," Kit challenged. "But now you're just a pawn in Dooku's game."

"I wield great power, Jedi fool!" Grievous laughed.

With lightning-quick strikes, Kit moved in on the general. He skillfully disarmed Grievous of one of his lightsabers. It spun through the air and landed in Kit's hand. Kit looked down at the lightsaber hilt—it was Nahdar's.

"That power will only consume you." Kit smiled as he ignited the second lightsaber and attacked Grievous with dual strikes.

The Jedi Master's expertise began to drive Grievous back. He maneuvered quickly, flipping and blocking Grievous's attacks with great skill. Grievous was on the retreat when the MagnaGuards appeared on the landing. Kit was quickly backed to the ledge.

"How quickly power can change hands." Grievous chuckled as he stood tall. "Surrender and I promise that you will die swiftly."

Kit lowered and then deactivated his lightsaber. He appeared to be defeated. Grievous looked at him victoriously, but Kit just smiled and flipped backward off the ledge of the landing and onto the wing of his awaiting starfighter.

He could hear Grievous howl, "Stop him!" as he climbed into the cockpit of his starfighter. Kit knew that there was nothing that the MagnaGuards could do but watch as he flew off.

"Let's go home, Arsix," Kit said sadly as the smile faded from his face.

Grievous stood on the ledge and watched as Kit's starfighter vanished into the fog. As if on cue, a hologram of Count Dooku appeared behind him.

Grievous turned to face his Master. "Count Dooku," he said. "The Jedi have been defeated."

"Victory over the clones and the young Jedi were to be expected," Dooku replied. "But to beat a member of the Jedi Council, this is truly an accomplishment worthy of recognition."

Grievous stood silently for a moment, both embarrassed and angry. "The Jedi Fisto escaped," he eventually spoke.

Dooku just stared at him. He wasn't impressed.

"There's always room for improvement," the count added as the hologram faded away.

Grievous let out a frustrated roar. He knew that he had failed his Master.

Back on Coruscant, Kit made his way to the chambers of the Jedi High Council. He had been summoned by Masters Yoda and Mace Windu. They were curious for a report on the Jedi's mission. As Master Windu asked him of the fate of his former Padawan, Kit just looked down at the second lightsaber hanging from his belt and thought of his friend, Nahdar.

"His heart was in the right place," Kit said solemnly. "But he tried to answer Grievous's power with his own."

Master Yoda looked at him with understanding as he replied, "To answer power with power, the Jedi way is not. In this war, a danger there is . . . of losing who we are."